Moonflower Murders

Also available by Anthony Horowitz

The House of Silk
Moriarty
Trigger Mortis
Magpie Murders
The Word is Murder
Forever and a Day
The Sentence is Death

ANTHONY HOROWITZ

Moonflower Murders

CENTURY

5 7 9 10 8 6 4

Century
20 Vauxhall Bridge Road
London SW1V 2SA

Century is part of the Penguin Random House group of companies
whose addresses can be found at global.penguinrandomhouse.com.

Copyright © Anthony Horowitz 2020

Anthony Horowitz has asserted his right to be identified as the author
of this Work in accordance with the Copyright, Designs and Patents Act 1988.

First published by Century in 2020

www.penguin.co.uk

A CIP catalogue record for this book is available from the British Library.

ISBN 9781529124347 (hardback)
ISBN 9781529124354 (trade paperback)

Typeset in 13.5/16.5 pt Fournier MT Std
by Integra Software Services Pvt. Ltd, Pondicherry

Printed and bound in Great Britain by Clays Ltd, Elcograf S.p.A.

Penguin Random House is committed to a sustainable future for
our business, our readers and our planet. This book is made from
Forest Stewardship Council® certified paper.

For Eric Hamlish and Jan Salindar – with thanks for so
many good times

Moonflower
Murders

Agios Nikolaos, Crete

The Polydorus is a charming family-run hotel, located a short walk away from the lively town of Agios Nikolaos, one hour from Heraklion. Rooms cleaned daily, all with Wi-Fi and air con, some with sea views. Coffee and home-cooked meals served on our lovely terraces. Visit our website or find us on booking.com.

You have no idea how long it took me to write that. I was worried about so many adjectives bunching up together. Was 'lively' the right word to describe Agios Nikolaos? I'd started with 'busy' but then decided it might suggest the endless traffic and noise that were very much part of the place too. We were actually fifteen minutes from the town centre. Was that a 'short walk'? Should I have mentioned Ammoudi beach next door?

The funny thing is, I spent almost all my working life as an editor and I never had any problem dealing with writers' manuscripts, but when it came to a four-line advertisement on the back of a postcard I sweated over every syllable. In the end, I handed it to Andreas who read it in about five seconds

1

and then just grunted and nodded, which, after all the trouble I'd taken, both pleased and infuriated me at the same time. That's something I've noticed about the Greeks. They're an incredibly emotional people. Their drama, poetry and music go straight to the heart. But when it comes to everyday business, to the little details, they prefer things to be '*siga siga*', which translates roughly as 'Who gives a damn?' It was a phrase I heard every day.

Examining what I'd written along with a cigarette and a cup of strong black coffee, two thoughts crossed my mind. We were going to put the cards in a rack beside the reception desk, but since tourists would already be in the hotel when they picked them up, what exactly was the point? And more pertinently, what the hell was I doing here? How had I allowed my life to come to this?

Just two years away from my fiftieth birthday, at a time when I had thought I would be enjoying all the comforts of life that come with a reasonable income, a small flat in London and a full social diary, I had found myself the co-owner and manager of a hotel that was actually much nicer than I'd managed to describe. Polydorus was right on the edge of the water, with two terraces shaded from the sun by umbrellas and cypress trees. It had just twelve rooms, a young, local staff who were always cheerful even at their most haphazard, and a loyal clientele. We had simple food, Mythos lager, an in-house musician and perfect views. The sort of travellers we encouraged wouldn't dream of arriving on one of those gigantic coaches I would watch inching along roads that had never been designed to accommodate them, on their way to the six-storey monstrosities on the other side of the bay.

What we also had, unfortunately, was dodgy wiring, impossible plumbing and intermittent Wi-Fi. I don't want to slip into lazy Greek stereotyping and maybe I was just unlucky, but reliability was hardly a watchword amongst the people we employed. Panos was an excellent chef but if he argued with his wife, his children or his motorbike he would be a no-show and Andreas would have to take over in the kitchen, leaving me to host the bar and restaurant, which might be full but without any waiters or half-empty with too many of them. Somehow a happy compromise never seemed to materialise. There was always a faint possibility that a supplier might actually arrive on time but it would never be with the goods that we had actually ordered. If anything broke – and everything did – we would have hours of nervous tension waiting to see if the mechanic or engineer would show up.

For the most part our guests seemed happy. But we were running about like actors in one of those madcap French farces trying to make it all look seamless and by the time I collapsed into bed, often at one or two in the morning, I was so exhausted that I lay there feeling almost desiccated, like a mummy in a shroud. That was when I would be at my lowest, falling asleep with the knowledge that the moment I opened my eyes the whole thing would start all over again.

I'm being too negative. Of course it was wonderful too. The Aegean sunset is like nothing you will see anywhere in the world and I would watch it every evening, staring in wonder. No wonder the Greeks believed in gods – Helios in his golden chariot blazing across that enormous sky, the Lasithiotika mountains transformed into strips of the thinnest gauze, first pink, then mauve, darkening and fading at the same time. I swam at seven o'clock every morning, washing away in the crystal sea the traces of too much wine and cigarette smoke. There were dinners in tiny tavernas in Fourni and Limnes with the smell of jasmine, the stars twinkling, raucous laughter, the clink of raki glasses. I'd even started to learn Greek, working three hours a week with a girl young enough to be my daughter who managed to take the stressed syllables and verbs that weren't just irregular but downright indecent and somehow make them fun.

But this wasn't a holiday for me. I'd come to Greece after the catastrophe that was *Magpie Murders*. It was the last book I'd worked on and it had led to the death of the author, the collapse of my publishing company and the end of my career … in that order. There had been nine Atticus Pünd novels, all of them bestsellers, and I had thought there would be many more. But that was all over now. Instead, I found myself starting a new life, and frankly too much of it was hard work.

Inevitably, this had had an effect on my relationship with Andreas. The two of us didn't quarrel – we weren't the quarrelling sort – but we'd developed a way of communicating that had become increasingly terse and wary, circling each other like two prize boxers who have no intention of starting the fight. In fact, a full-throttle punch-up might have done us both good. We had managed to drift into that awful arena, so familiar to the long-term married couple, where what was left unspoken was actually more damaging than what was said. We weren't married, by the way. Andreas had proposed to me, doing the whole diamond-ring-down-on-one-knee thing, but we had both been too busy to follow through, and anyway, my Greek wasn't good enough yet to understand the service. We had decided to wait.

Time had done us no favours. In London, Andreas had always been my best friend. Perhaps it was because we weren't living together that I had always looked forward to seeing him. We read the same books. We loved eating in ... especially when Andreas cooked. We had great sex. But Crete had trapped us in an altogether different sort of arrangement and even though it had only been a couple of years since we had left the UK, I was already thinking about a way out, even if I wasn't actively looking for one.

I didn't need to. The way out arrived early one Monday morning with a smart-looking couple, obviously English, walking arm in arm down the slope that led from the main road. I could tell at once that they were rich and that they weren't here on holiday. He was wearing a jacket and long trousers – ridiculous for the morning heat – a polo shirt and a panama hat. She had on the sort of dress that was more suited to a tennis party than the beach, a proper necklace and carried a neat little clutch bag. Both had expensive sunglasses. I guessed they were in their sixties.

The man came into the bar and uncoupled himself from his wife. I saw him examining me. 'Excuse me,' he said in a cultivated voice. 'Do you speak English?'

'Yes.'

'I don't suppose ... you wouldn't by any chance be Susan Ryeland?'

'That's me.'

'I wonder if I might have a word with you, Miss Ryeland? My name is Lawrence Treherne. This is my wife, Pauline.'

'How do you do.' Pauline Treherne smiled at me but not in a friendly way. She didn't trust me and she hadn't even met me yet.

'Can I get you a coffee?' I phrased the question carefully. I wasn't offering to buy them one. I don't want to give the impression that I'm mean, but this was something else preying on my mind. I had sold my flat in north London and ploughed most of my savings into Polydorus, but so far I hadn't made any profit. Quite the reverse: although I'm not sure that Andreas and I were doing anything wrong, we had still managed to find ourselves almost ten thousand euros in debt. Our funds were leaking away and I sometimes felt that the distance between me and bankruptcy could be measured by the froth on a free cappuccino.

'No. We're all right, thank you.'

I steered them towards one of the tables in the bar. The terrace was already crowded, but Vangelis, who worked as a waiter when he wasn't playing his guitar, was managing fine and it was cooler out of the heat. 'So how can I help you, Mr Treherne?'

'Lawrence, please.' He took off the hat, revealing thinning silver hair and a scalp that had still managed to catch the sun. He placed the hat in front of him. 'I hope you'll forgive us for tracking you down. We have a mutual friend – Sajid Khan. He sends you his regards, by the way.'

Sajid Khan? It took me a moment to remember that he was a solicitor, living in the Suffolk town of Framlingham. He had been a friend of Alan Conway, the author of *Magpie Murders*. When Alan died, Sajid Khan was the one who had discovered the body. But I'd only met him a couple of times. I wouldn't have called him a friend, mutual or otherwise.

'Do you live in Suffolk?' I asked.

'Yes. We own a hotel near Woodbridge. Mr Khan has helped us on one or two occasions.' Lawrence hesitated, suddenly uncomfortable. 'I was speaking to him last week about a rather difficult matter and he suggested we talk to you.'

I wondered how Khan had known I was here in Crete. Someone else must have told him because I certainly hadn't. 'You came all this way to talk to me?' I asked.

'It's not really that far and we travel quite a bit anyway. We're staying at the Minos Beach.' He pointed in the direction of his hotel, which was on the other side of a tennis court, right next to mine. It confirmed my first opinion that the Trehernes were rich. The Minos Beach was a boutique hotel with private villas and a garden full of sculptures. It cost around three hundred pounds a night. 'I did think about ringing,' he went on. 'But it's not something I'd want to discuss over the phone.'

This was getting more mysterious – and, frankly, annoying – by the minute. A four-hour flight from Stansted. A one-hour drive from Heraklion. Getting here had hardly been a stroll. 'What is this about?' I asked.

'It's about a murder.'

That last word hung in the air for a moment. On the other side of the terrace, the sun was shining. A bunch of local children were laughing and shouting, splashing about in the Aegean. Families were packed together around the tables.

7

I watched Vangelis go past with a tray laden with orange juice and iced coffee.

'What murder?' I asked.

'A man called Frank Parris. You won't have heard of him but you might know the hotel where the murder took place. It's called Branlow Hall.'

'And that's your hotel.'

'Yes. It is.' It was Pauline Treherne who answered, speaking for the first time. She sounded like a minor royal, cutting each word as if with a pair of scissors before allowing it to escape. And yet I got the feeling that she was as middle class as I was.

'He had booked in for three nights,' Lawrence said. 'He was killed on the second.'

A host of different questions were going through my mind. Who was Frank Parris? Who killed him? Why should I care? But I didn't say that. 'When did this happen?' I asked.

'About eight years ago,' Lawrence Treherne said.

Pauline Treherne set her clutch bag on the table, next to the panama hat, as if it was some agreed signal for her to take over. There was something about her – the way she used silence, her lack of emotion – that made me think she was always the one who made the important decisions. Her sunglasses were so dark that as she spoke to me I found myself almost transfixed by two images of myself listening.

'It might help if I tell you the entire story,' she said in that grating voice of hers. 'That way, you'll understand why we're here. I take it you're not too pressed for time?'

I had about fifty things I needed to be doing. 'Not at all,' I said.

'Thank you.' She collected herself. 'Frank Parris worked in advertising,' she began. 'He'd just come back to England from Australia, where he'd lived for several years. He was killed very brutally in his hotel room on the night of June the fifteenth, 2008. I'll always remember the date because it coincided with the wedding weekend of our daughter, Cecily.'

'Was he a guest?'

'No. We'd never met him. We'd taken over a dozen or so rooms for the wedding. We put up close family and friends. The hotel has thirty-two rooms in total and we'd decided, against my better judgement – my husband, I'm afraid, did not agree – to stay open to the public. Mr Parris was in Suffolk visiting relatives. He'd booked in for three nights. He was killed late on Friday night, although the body wasn't discovered until Saturday afternoon.'

'After the wedding,' Lawrence Treherne muttered.

'How was he killed?'

'He was struck several times with a hammer. His face was very badly disfigured and but for his wallet and his passport, which was found in his safe, the police would have been unable to identify him.'

'Cecily was most dreadfully upset,' Lawrence cut in. 'Well, we all were. It had been such a beautiful day. We had the wedding service in the garden and then lunch for a hundred guests. We couldn't have asked for better weather. And all the time, we were unaware that in a room actually overlooking the marquee, he'd been lying there in a pool of his own blood.'

'Cecily and Aiden had to postpone their honeymoon,' Pauline added, a tremor of indignation still there in her voice even after all these years. 'The police wouldn't allow them to leave. They said there was no question of it even though it was clear the murder had nothing to do with them.'

'Aiden is her husband?'

'Aiden MacNeil. Yes. Our son-in-law. They were meant to be leaving on the Sunday morning for Antigua, but in the end it was two weeks before they were allowed to go and by then the police had arrested the killer, so there was really no need for such a long delay.'

'So they knew who did it,' I said.

'Oh yes. It was all very straightforward,' Lawrence explained. 'It was actually someone we employed, a Romanian by the name of Stefan Codrescu. He was working as a general maintenance man and he lived in the hotel. He actually had a criminal record – we knew that when we employed him. In fact, it was rather the point, I'm afraid to say.' His eyes flickered downwards. 'My wife and I used to run a programme at the hotel. We employed young offenders – in the kitchen, cleaning, gardening – after they were released. We're great believers in prison reform and giving young men and women a second chance. I'm sure you're aware that the reoffending rate is astronomical. That's because these people don't get a chance to integrate themselves back into society. We worked closely with the probation service and they assured us that Stefan would be suitable for our programme.' He sighed heavily. 'They were wrong.'

'Cecily believed in him,' Pauline said.

'She knew him?'

'We have two daughters and they both work with us at the hotel. Cecily was the general manager when all this happened. In fact, she was the one who interviewed Stefan and employed him.'

'She got married at the same hotel where she worked?'

'Absolutely. It's a family business. Our staff are part of our family. She wouldn't think of having it anywhere else,' Pauline said.

'And she thought Stefan was innocent.'

'To begin with, yes. She insisted on it. That's the trouble with Cecily. She's always been far too good-natured, too trusting, the sort who believes the best in everyone. But the evidence against Stefan was overwhelming. I don't know where to begin. There were no fingerprints on the hammer … it had been wiped clean. But there was blood splatter on his clothes and on money – taken from the dead man – under his mattress. He was seen entering Frank Parris's room. And anyway, he confessed. When that happened, even Cecily had to admit that she was wrong and that was the end of it. She and Aiden went to Antigua. The hotel slowly returned to normal, although it took a long, long time and no one ever stayed in room twelve again. We use it for storage now. As I said, this all happened years ago and we thought it was behind us. But it seems not.'

'So what happened?' I asked. I was intrigued, despite myself.

Lawrence took over. 'Stefan was sentenced to life in prison and he's still behind bars. Cecily wrote to him a couple of times but he never replied and I thought she'd forgotten him. She seemed perfectly happy running the hotel and also, of course, being with Aiden. She was twenty-six when they got married. Two years older than him. She'll be thirty-four next month.'

'Do they have any children?'

'Yes. A little girl. Well, she's seven now ... Roxana.'

'Our first granddaughter.' Pauline's voice faltered. 'She's a lovely child, everything we could have ever wanted.'

'Pauline and I are semi-retired,' Lawrence went on. 'We have a house near Hyères in the South of France and we spend quite a bit of time down there. Anyway, a few days ago, Cecily rang us. I took the call. This would have been around two o'clock, French time. I could tell at once that Cecily sounded very upset. More than that, I'd say she was nervous. I don't know where she was calling from, but this was a Tuesday so she was probably at the hotel. We normally have a bit of banter but she got straight to the point. She said she'd been thinking about what happened—'

'The murder.'

'Exactly. She said that she had been right all along and that Stefan Codrescu was not responsible for the crime. I asked her what she was talking about and she said she'd come across something in a book she'd been given. "It was right there – staring me in the face." Those were her exact words. Anyway, she told me she'd already sent it to me and sure enough, it turned up the very next day.'

He reached into his jacket pocket and took out a paperback. I recognised it at once – the picture on the cover, the typeface, the title – and at that moment, this entire meeting began to make sense.

The book was *Atticus Pünd Takes the Case*, number three in the series written by Alan Conway that I had edited and published. I immediately recalled that it was largely set in a hotel, but in the county of Devon, not in Suffolk, and in

1953, not the present day. I remembered the launch party at the German embassy in London. Alan had had too much to drink and had insulted the ambassador.

'Alan knew about the murder?' I asked.

'Oh yes. He came to the hotel and stayed a few nights, six weeks after it happened. We both met him. He told us that he had been a friend of the dead man, Frank Parris, and he asked us a lot of questions about the murder. He talked to our staff as well. We had absolutely no idea that he was going to turn the whole thing into an entertainment. If he'd been honest with us, we might have been more circumspect.'

Which was exactly the reason he wasn't honest with you, I thought.

'You never read the book?' I said.

'We forgot all about it,' Lawrence admitted. 'And Mr Conway certainly never sent us a copy.' He paused. 'But Cecily read it and she found something that cast new light on what had happened at Branlow Hall ... at least, that's what she believed.' He glanced at his wife as if seeking her approbation. 'Pauline and I have both read the book and we can't see any connection.'

'There are similarities,' Pauline said. 'Firstly, nearly all the characters are recognisable, clearly based on people that Mr Conway met in Woodbridge. They even have the same names ... or very similar ones. But what I don't understand is that he seems to have taken pleasure in twisting people so that they come out like horrible caricatures of themselves. The owners of the Moonflower, which is the hotel in the book, are clearly based on Lawrence and myself, for example. But they're both crooks. Why would he do that? We've never done anything dishonest in our lives.' She seemed more indignant than upset. The way she was looking at me, it was almost as if I was to blame.

'In answer to your question, we had no idea the book had been published,' she went on. 'I don't read murder mysteries myself. Neither of us does. Sajid Khan told us that Mr Conway is no longer alive. Maybe that's just as well because if he were, we might be very tempted to take legal action.'

'So let me get this straight,' I said. I had the sense of facts tumbling on top of each other, yet I knew there was something they hadn't told me. 'You believe that maybe, despite all the evidence, not to mention the confession, Stefan Codrescu did not kill Frank Parris and that Alan Conway came to the hotel and discovered — in a matter of days — who the real killer was. He then somehow identified that person in *Atticus Pünd Takes the Case.*'

'Exactly.'

'But that makes no sense at all, Pauline. If he knew the killer and there was an innocent man in prison, surely Alan would have gone straight to the police! Why would he turn it into a work of fiction?'

'That's precisely why we're here, Susan. From what Sajid Khan told us, you knew Alan Conway better than anyone. You edited the book. If there is something in there, I can't think of anyone more likely to find it.'

'Wait a minute.' Suddenly I knew what was missing. 'This all started when your daughter spotted something in *Atticus Pünd Takes the Case.* Was she the only one who read it before she sent it to you?'

'I don't know.'

14

'But what was it she saw? Why didn't you just call her and ask her what she meant?'

It was Lawrence Treherne who answered my question. 'Of course we called her,' he said. 'We both read the book and then we rang her several times from France. Finally we got through to Aiden and he told us what had happened.' He paused. 'It seems that our daughter has disappeared.'

Departure

I lost my temper with Andreas that evening. I really didn't mean to but the day had brought so many mishaps, one after another, that I was going to scream either at the moon or at him and he just happened to be nearer.

It had begun with that nice couple Bruce and Brenda from Macclesfield, who turned out not to be that nice after all, demanding a fifty per cent reduction in their bill or they were going to hit TripAdvisor with a list of complaints that they'd stacked up from the day they'd arrived and which, they assured us, would put anyone off ever coming anywhere near us again. And what was their problem? An hour without Wi-Fi. The sound of guitar music at night. The sighting of a solitary cockroach. What annoyed me was they had complained every morning, always with tight little smiles, and I'd known all along that they were going to try something on. I'd developed an antenna for the tourists who arrived with extortion as part of their holiday plans. You'd be amazed how many of them there were.

Panos didn't show up. Vangelis was late. Andreas's computer had a glitch – I'd asked him to get it looked at – and it had managed to send two room requests into spam. By the time we noticed, the clients had booked elsewhere. Before we went to bed, we had a glass of Metaxa, the Greek brandy that only tastes nice in Greece, but I was still in a bad mood and it was when Andreas asked me what the matter was that I finally snapped.

'What do you think is the fucking matter, Andreas? Everything!'

I don't usually swear . . . at least, not at people I like. Lying in bed, watching Andreas getting undressed, I was annoyed with myself. Part of me wanted to blame him for everything that had happened since I'd come to Crete, while another part blamed myself for letting him down. But the worst of it was the sense of helplessness – that events had taken over and I was being steered by them rather than the other way round. Had I really chosen a life where complete strangers could humiliate me for a few euros and where my entire well-being could be decided by a lost reservation?

Right then I knew I had to go back to England and that actually I'd known it for some time, even if I'd tried to pretend otherwise.

Andreas cleaned his teeth and came out of the bathroom naked, which is how he slept, looking every inch like one of those figures – an ephebe or a satyr perhaps – that you might see on the side of an ancient vase. And it did seem to me that he had become more Greek in the past couple of years. His black hair was a little shaggier, his eyes a little darker and he had a sort of swagger that I'm sure he'd never displayed when he was teaching at Westminster School. He'd put on some weight too – or perhaps it was just that I noticed his stomach more now that he was out of a suit. He was still a handsome man. I was still attracted to him. But suddenly I needed to be away from him.

I waited until he got into bed. We slept under a single sheet with the windows open. We hardly got any mosquitoes right next to the sea and I preferred the night air to the artificial chill of the air conditioning.

'Andreas . . . ' I said.

'What?' He would have fallen asleep in seconds if I'd let him. His voice was already drowsy.

'I want to go back to London.'

'What?' He twisted round, propping himself up on his elbow. 'What do you mean?'

'There's something I have to do.'

'In London?'

'No. I have to go to Suffolk.' He was looking at me, his face full of concern. 'I won't be long,' I said. 'Just a couple of weeks.'

'We need you here, Susan.'

'We need money, Andreas. We're not going to be able to pay our bills if we don't get some extra finance. And I've been offered a great deal of money to do a job. Ten thousand pounds. Cash!'

*

It was true.

After the Trehernes had told me about the murder at their hotel, they had gone on to explain how their daughter had disappeared.

'It's very unlike her to wander off without telling anyone,' Lawrence had said. 'And certainly to leave her daughter behind . . . '

'Who's looking after the child?' I asked.

'Aiden's there. And there's a nanny.'

'It's not "unlike" her.' Pauline gave her husband the most withering of scowls. 'She's never done anything like this in her life, and of course she wouldn't leave Roxana on her own.' She turned to me. 'We're worried sick, if you want the truth, Susan. And Lawrence may not agree, but I'm convinced it's got something to do with this book.'

'I do agree!' Lawrence muttered.

'Did anyone else know about her concerns?' I asked.

'I already told you that she telephoned us from Branlow Hall, so any one of a number of people could have overheard her.'

'I mean, had she talked about her suspicions with anyone else?'

Pauline Treherne shook her head. 'We tried several times to phone her from France and when she didn't answer we called Aiden. He hadn't rung because he didn't want to worry us, but it turned out that he had contacted the police the same day she disappeared. Unfortunately, they didn't take him very seriously . . . at least, not to begin with. They suggested the two of them might be having marriage difficulties.'

'And were they?'

'Not at all,' Lawrence said. 'They've always been very happy together. The police spoke to Eloise – she's the nanny – and she said the same. She never heard any arguments.'

'Aiden's a perfect son-in-law. He's clever and he's hard-working. I only wish Lisa could find someone like him. And he's as worried as we are!'

All the time Pauline had been speaking to me, I'd thought she was fighting something. Suddenly she pulled out a packet of cigarettes and lit one. She smoked like someone who had just taken up the habit again after a long abstinence. She inhaled, then went on.

'By the time we got back to England, the police had finally decided to take an interest. Not that they were very much help. Cecily had taken the dog for a walk. She has a shaggy golden retriever called Bear – we've always kept dogs. She left the hotel at about three o'clock in the afternoon and parked the car at Woodbridge station. She often used to take the river path. That's the River Deben. There's a circular walk that takes you along the edge and to begin with it's well populated. But then it becomes wilder and more remote until you come to a wood and on the other side there's a road that takes you back through Martlesham.'

'So if someone attacked her—'

'It's not the sort of thing that ever happens in Suffolk. But yes, there were plenty of places where she would have been on her own, out of sight.' Pauline took a breath and went on. 'Aiden got worried when she didn't come home for dinner and quite rightly called the police. Two uniformed officers came round and asked a few questions, but they didn't raise the alarm until the next morning, which was much too late of course. By that time Bear had shown up, on his own, back at the station, and after that they took everything more seriously. They had people – and their own dogs – out searching the entire area from Martlesham all the way back to Melton. But it was no good. There are fields, woods, mudflats ... a lot of ground to cover. They didn't find anything.'

'How long is it since she went missing?' I asked.

'The last time anyone saw her was last Wednesday.'

I felt the silence fall. Five days. That was a long time, an abyss into which Cecily had fallen.

'You've come all this way to talk to me,' I said, finally. 'What exactly do you want me to do?'

Pauline glanced at her husband.

'The answer is in this book,' he explained. '*Atticus Pünd Takes the Case*. You must know it better than anyone.'

'Actually, it's been quite a few years since I read it,' I admitted.

'You worked with the author, this man, Alan Conway. You knew how his mind worked. If we were to ask you to reread it, I'm sure there are things that might occur to you that we haven't noticed. And if you actually came to Branlow Hall and read the book in situ, so to speak, maybe you might see what it was that our daughter spotted and why she felt compelled to ring us. And that in turn might tell us where she is or what's happened to her.'

His voice faltered as he spoke those last words. *What's happened to her*. There might be a simple reason why she had vanished but it was unlikely. She knew something. She was a danger to someone. The thought was better left unsaid.

'Can I have one of these?' I asked. I helped myself to one of Pauline Treherne's cigarettes. My own pack was behind the bar. The whole ritual – pulling out the cigarette, lighting it, taking the first puff – gave me time to think. 'I can't come to England,' I said eventually. 'I'm afraid I'm too busy here. But I will read the book if you don't mind leaving me your copy. I can't promise anything will come to mind. I mean, I remember the story and it doesn't correspond quite with what you've told me. But I can email you—'

'No. That won't do.' Pauline had already made up her mind. 'You need to talk to Aiden and Lisa – and Eloise, for that matter. And you should meet Derek, the night manager. He was on duty the night Frank Parris was killed and spoke to the detective in charge. He's in Alan Conway's book too – although he's called Eric.' She leaned towards me, imploring. 'We're not asking you for a lot of your time.'

'And we'll pay you,' Lawrence added. 'We have plenty of money and we're not going to hold back if it helps find our daughter.' He paused. 'Ten thousand pounds?'

That drew a sharp look from his wife and it occurred to me that, without thinking, he had greatly increased, perhaps doubled, the amount they had intended to offer me. That was what my reluctance had done. I thought for a moment that she was going to say something, but she relaxed and nodded.

Ten thousand pounds. I thought about the replastering on the balcony. A new computer for Andreas. The ice-cream display chest that was on the blink. Panos and Vangelis, who had both been muttering about pay rises.

*

'How could I say no?' This was what I told Andreas now in our bedroom, late at night. 'We need the money, and anyway, maybe I can help them find their daughter.'

'You think she's still alive?'

'It's possible. But if she isn't, perhaps I can find out who killed her.'

Andreas sat up. He was wide awake now and he was worried about me. I felt bad that I had sworn at him. 'The last time you went looking for a killer, it didn't end very well,' he reminded me.

'This is different. This isn't personal. It's got nothing to do with me.'

'Which sounds to me like an argument for leaving it alone.'

'You may be right. But ... '

I had made up my mind and Andreas knew it.

'I need a break anyway,' I said. 'It's been two years, Andreas, and apart from a weekend in Santorini we haven't been anywhere. I'm completely worn out, endlessly firefighting, endlessly trying to make things work. I thought you'd understand.'

'A break from the hotel or a break from me?' he asked.

I wasn't sure I had an answer to that.

'Where will you stay?' he asked.

'With Katie. It'll be nice.' I rested a hand on his arm, feeling the warm flesh and the curve of his muscle. 'You can manage perfectly well without me. I'll ask Nell to come in and look after things. And we'll talk to each other every day.'

'I don't want you to go, Susan.'

'But you're not going to stop me, Andreas.'

He paused and in that moment I could see him fighting with himself. My Andreas versus Andreas the Greek. 'No,' he said, finally. 'You must do what you have to.'

*

Two days later, he drove me to Heraklion airport. There are parts of the road from Agios Nikolaos – as you pass Neapoli and Latsida – that are actually very beautiful. The landscape is wild and empty, with the mountains stretching into the distance and the sense that nothing very much has been touched for a thousand years. Even the new motorway after Malia is surrounded by gorgeous countryside and as you draw nearer you dip down and find yourself close to a wide, white sand beach. Maybe that was what gave me a sense of sadness, an understanding of what I was leaving behind. Suddenly I wasn't thinking of all the problems and the chores of running Polydorus. I was thinking of midnight and the waves and *pansélinos* – the full moon. Wine. Laughter. My peasant life.

When I'd been preparing to leave, I'd deliberately chosen my smallest bag. I'd thought it would be a statement to Andreas and to myself that this was just a brief business trip and that I would be home very soon. But going through my wardrobe, looking at clothes that I hadn't worn for two years, I found myself piling things up on the bed. I was going back to an English summer, which meant that it could be hot and cold, wet and dry, all in one day. I would be staying in a posh country hotel. They probably had a dress code for dinner. And I was being paid ten thousand pounds. I needed to look professional.

So by the time I arrived at Heraklion airport, I found myself dragging my old wheelie behind me, the actual wheels squeaking malevolently as they spun against the concrete floor. The two of us stood for a moment in the harsh air conditioning and the harsher electric light of the departure lounge.

He took hold of me. 'Promise me you'll look after yourself. And call me when you get there. We can FaceTime.'

'If the Wi-Fi isn't on the blink!'

'Promise me, Susan.'

'I promise.'

He held me with both hands on my arms and kissed me. I smiled at him, then trailed my suitcase over to the stout, scowling Greek girl in her blue uniform who checked my passport and boarding card before allowing me through to security. I turned and waved.

But Andreas had already gone.

Cuttings

It was quite a shock being back in London. After so much time in Agios Nikolaos, which wasn't very much more than an overgrown fishing village, I found myself consumed by the city and I was unprepared for the intensity of it, the noise, the number of people in the streets. Everything was greyer than I remembered and it was hard to cope with the dust and petrol fumes in the air. The amount of new construction also made my head spin. Views that I had known all my working life had disappeared in the space of two years. London's various mayors, with their love of tall buildings, had allowed different architects to gouge their initials into the skyline with the result that everything was both familiar and alien at the same time. Sitting in the back of a black cab, being driven along the River Thames on the way from the airport, the cluster of new flats and offices around Battersea Power Station looked to me like a battlefield. It was as if there had been an invasion and all those cranes with their blinking red lights were monstrous birds, picking over carcasses lying unseen on the ground.

I had decided to spend the first night in a hotel, which was, frankly, weird. A lifelong Londoner, I had somehow degenerated into a tourist and I hated the hotel, a Premier Inn in Farringdon, not because there was anything wrong with it – it was perfectly clean and comfortable – but because that was where I was forced to stay. Sitting on the bed with its mauve cushions and 'sleeping moon' logo, I felt perfectly miserable. I was already missing Andreas. I had texted him from the airport but I knew that if I FaceTimed him I would probably end up crying and that would prove he was right, I should never have gone. The sooner I was in Suffolk, the better. But I wasn't ready to make the journey yet. There were one or two things I had to do.

After an intermittent sleep and a breakfast – egg, sausage, bacon, beans – that looked identical to every breakfast ever served in a cut-price hotel chain, I strolled over to King's Cross to one of the storage depots built into the arches under the railway lines. When I moved to Crete, I had sold my flat in Crouch End and almost everything in it, but at the last moment I had decided to hang on to my car, a bright red MGB Roadster which I had bought in the moment of madness that had coincided with my fortieth birthday. I had never thought I would drive it again and storing it had been a crazy extravagance; I was paying £150 a month for the privilege. But I just couldn't bring myself to get rid of it and now, as it was wheeled out for me by two young men, it was like being reunited with an old friend. More than that. It was a part of my former life that I had back again. Just sinking into the cracked leather of the driver's seat with the wooden steering wheel and absurdly old-fashioned radio above my knees made me feel better about myself. If I did go back to Crete, I decided, I would drive there and to hell with the problems of Greek registration and left-hand drive. I turned the key and the engine started first time. I pumped the accelerator a few times, enjoying the growl of welcome that came from the engine, then drove off, heading down the Euston Road.

It was midmorning and the traffic wasn't too bad, which is to say that it was actually moving. I didn't want to go straight back to the hotel so I drove around London, taking in a few sights just for the hell of it. Euston Station was being rebuilt. Gower Street was as shabby as ever. I don't suppose it was coincidence that brought me into Bloomsbury, the area behind the British Museum, but without really thinking about it, I found myself outside Cloverleaf Books, the independent publishing house where I had worked for eleven years. Or what was left of it. The building was an eyesore, boarded-up windows and charred bricks surrounded by scaffolding, and it occurred to me that the insurers must be refusing to pay out. Perhaps arson and attempted murder hadn't been included in the policy.

I thought of driving out to Crouch End, giving the MG a good run for its money – but that would have been too dispiriting. Anyway, I had work to do. I put the car into an NCP in Farringdon, then walked back to the hotel. I didn't need to check out until noon, which gave me an hour alone with the coffee machine, two packets of complimentary biscuits and the Internet. I opened up my laptop and began a series of searches: Branlow Hall, Stefan Codrescu, Frank Parris, murder.

These were the articles I found: a murder mystery stripped of its intrigue and told in just four indifferent chapters.

The *East Anglian Daily Times*: 18 JUNE 2008
MAN KILLED AT CELEBRITY HOTEL

Police are investigating the murder of a 53-year-old man after his body was discovered in the five-star hotel where he was staying. Branlow Hall, located close to Woodbridge in Suffolk, charges £300 a night for an executive suite and is a much sought-after venue for celebrity weddings and parties. It has also been used as a location for many television series, including ITV's *Endeavour*, *Top Gear* and *Antiques Roadshow*.

The victim has been identified as Frank Parris, a well-known figure in the advertising industry who won awards for his work on Barclays Bank and for the LGBT rights organisation, Stonewall. He rose to be creative director of McCann Erickson in London before moving to Australia to set up his own agency. He was unmarried.

Detective Superintendent Richard Locke, who is heading the investigation, said: 'This was a particularly brutal murder that would seem to have been carried out by a single individual with the motive of theft. Money belonging to Mr Parris has been recovered and we expect to make an arrest shortly.'

The murder took place on the night before the wedding of Aiden MacNeil and Cecily Treherne, whose parents, Lawrence and Pauline Treherne, own the hotel.

The body was discovered shortly after the ceremony, which had taken place in the hotel garden. Neither of the couples was available for comment.

The *East Anglian Daily Times*: 20 JUNE 2008
MAN HELD IN WOODBRIDGE KILLING

Police have arrested a 22-year-old man in connection with the brutal murder of a retired advertising executive at Branlow Hall, the well-known Suffolk hotel. Detective Superintendent Richard Locke, who is in charge of the investigation, said: 'This was a horrific crime, committed without any scruples. My team has worked quickly and very thoroughly and I am glad to say that we have been able to make an arrest. I have every sympathy for the young couple whose special day was ruined by these events.'

The suspect has been remanded in custody and is due to appear at Ipswich Crown Court next week.

The *Daily Mail*: 22 OCTOBER 2008
LIFE IMPRISONMENT FOR 'HAMMER HORROR' SUFFOLK KILLER

A Romanian migrant, Stefan Codrescu, was sentenced to life imprisonment at Ipswich Crown Court, following the murder of 53-year-old Frank Parris at the £300-a-night Branlow Hall hotel near Woodbridge, Suffolk. Parris, described as 'a brilliant creative mind', had recently returned from Australia and had been planning to retire.

Codrescu, who pleaded guilty, entered the UK when he was twelve years old and quickly came to the attention of London police investigating Romanian organised crime gangs involved in cloned credit cards, stolen UK passports and false identity documents. Aged nineteen, he was arrested for aggravated burglary and assault. He was sentenced to two years in jail.

Lawrence Treherne, the owner of Branlow Hall, was in court to hear the sentence. He had employed Codrescu, who had been at the hotel for five months, as part of an outreach programme for young offenders. Mr Treherne said that he did not regret his actions. 'My wife and I were shocked by the death of Mr Parris,' he said in a statement outside the court. 'But I still believe that it is right to give young people a second chance and to try to integrate them into society.'

But sentencing Codrescu to a minimum term of twenty-five years, Judge Azra Rashid said: 'Despite your background, you were given a unique opportunity to turn your life around. Instead, you betrayed the trust and goodwill of your employers and committed a brutal crime for financial gain.'

The court had heard that Codrescu, now 22, had racked up debts playing online poker and slot machines. Jonathan Clarke, defending, said that Codrescu had lost touch with reality. 'He was living in a virtual world with debts that were spiralling out of control.

What happened that night was a sort of madness ... a mental breakdown.'

Parris was attacked with a hammer and beaten so badly that he was unrecognisable. Detective Superintendent Richard Locke, who made the arrest, said that this was 'the most sickening case I have ever encountered'.

A spokesperson for Screen Counselling, a Norwich-based charity, has called on the gambling commission to ban online betting with credit cards.

That was the story: the beginning, the middle and the end. But trawling through the Internet, I came across what might have been a coda to the whole affair had it not actually predated everything that had occurred.

Campaign: 12 MAY 2008
LAST CALL FOR SYDNEY-BASED SUNDOWNER

Sundowner, the Sydney-based advertising agency set up by former McCann Erickson supremo Frank Parris, has gone out of business. The Australian Securities and Investments Commission – the country's official financial watchdog – confirmed that after just three years the agency has ceased to trade.

Parris, who began his career as a copywriter, was a well-known figure in the London advertising scene for more than two decades, winning awards for his work on Barclay's Bank and Domino's pizza. He created the controversial Action Fag campaign for Stonewall in 1997, promoting gay rights in the armed forces.

He was himself completely open about his sexuality and was well known for his extravagant and flamboyant parties. It has been suggested that his move to Australia was prompted by a decision to tone down his public image.

In its first month, Sundowner picked up some significant accounts, including Von Zipper sunglasses, Wagon Wheels and Kustom footwear. However, its early success took place against a subdued market that led to a significant shrinkage in consumer and advertising spending. Internet advertising and online videos are the fastest growing areas in Australia and it's clear that Sundowner, with its emphasis on traditional rather than digital media, had arrived too quickly at the last chance saloon.

So what was I to make of all this information?

Well, I suppose it was the editor in me that noticed that every single one of the reports had described the murder as brutal, as if anyone was ever murdered gently or with affection. The journalists had managed to sketch in the character of Frank Parris with what few details they had – award-winning, gay, extrovert, ultimately a failure. That hadn't stopped the *Mail* from characterising him as 'a brilliant creative mind', but then they would have been prepared to forgive him for almost anything. He had, after all, been murdered by a Romanian. Had Stefan Codrescu really been involved in gangs trading passports and credit cards, etc? There was no evidence of it and the fact that the police had been investigating Romanian gangs could have been entirely coincidental. He had, after all, been arrested for burglary.

As for the brilliant Frank Parris, there was something almost bizarre about his turning up in a hotel in Suffolk, particularly on the night of a wedding to which he had not been invited. Pauline Treherne had told me he was visiting relatives so why hadn't he stayed with them?

The mention of Detective Superintendent Richard Locke worried me. We had met following the death of Alan Conway and I think it's fair to say we had not got on. I remembered him – a big, angry police officer who had swept into a coffee shop on the outskirts of Ipswich, shouted at me for fifteen minutes and then left again. Alan had based a character on him and Locke had decided to blame me. It had taken him less than a week to identify Stefan as the culprit, arrest him and then charge him. Was he wrong? According to the newspaper stories and, for that matter, what the Trehernes had told me, the whole thing could hardly be more straightforward.

But eight years later, Cecily Treherne had thought otherwise. And she had disappeared.

There wasn't much more to do in London. It seemed obvious to me that I would have to talk to Stefan Codrescu, which meant visiting him in prison, but I didn't even know where he was being held and the Trehernes had been unable to help. How was I supposed to find out? I went back on the Internet but I didn't find anything there. Then I remembered an author I knew: Craig Andrews. He had come to writing late and I had published his first novel, a thriller set in the prison system. On first reading I had been impressed by the violence of his writing but also by its authenticity. He had done a lot of research.

Of course, he had another publisher now. Cloverleaf Books had rather let him down by going out of business and burning to the ground, but on the other hand the book had been a success and I had noticed a good review of his latest in the *Mail on Sunday*. I had nothing to lose so I sent him an email telling him that I was back in England and asking him if he could help me track down Stefan. I wasn't confident that he would reply.

After that, I packed up my laptop, grabbed my suitcase and rescued my MG from the car park, where it had already been charged a ridiculous sum of money for the grim, dusty corner where it had been housed. It still made me happy to see it. I got in and moments later I was roaring down the exit ramp and out onto the Farringdon Road, on my way to Suffolk.

Branlow Hall

I could have stayed with my sister while I was in Suffolk but the Trehernes had offered me free accommodation at their hotel and I had decided to accept. The truth was that I felt uncomfortable about spending too much time with Katie. She was two years younger than me and with her two adorable children, her lovely home, her successful husband and her circle of close friends, she could make me feel painfully inadequate, particularly when I looked at the haphazardness of my own life. After everything that had happened at Cloverleaf Books she had been delighted that I had flown off to Crete for what she saw as some sort of domestic normality and I didn't want to explain to her why I was back. It wasn't that she would judge me. It was more that I would feel myself being judged.

Anyway, it made more sense to base myself at the scene of the crime where so many of the witnesses would still be gathered. So I skirted Ipswich and made my way up the A12, passing the right turn that would have brought me into Woodbridge. Instead, I continued another five miles until I came to an expensive-looking sign (black paint, gold lettering) and a narrow lane that took me between hedgerows and bright red flecks of wild poppies to a stone gate and, on the other side, the ancestral home of the Branlow family, standing in a fair old slice of the Suffolk countryside.

So much of what I have to write about had either taken place or would take place here that I must describe it carefully.

It was a beautiful place, something between a country house, a castle and a French chateau, very square, surrounded by lawns dotted with ornamental trees and thicker woodland beyond. At some time in its history it might have been swivelled round because the gravel drive came in from the wrong direction, heading rather confusingly towards a side elevation with several windows but no door, while the actual entrance was round the corner, facing the other way.

It was when you stood here, in front of the house, that you appreciated its magnificence: the main door with its arched portico, the Gothic towers and crenellations, the coats of arms, and the stone chimneys that must have been connected to a multitude of fireplaces. The windows were double height with plaster heads of long-forgotten lords and ladies poking out of the corners. A number of stone birds perched high up on the very edge of the roof, with an eagle at each corner, and above the front door there was a rather fine owl with its wings outstretched. Now that I thought about it, I had seen an owl painted on the sign outside. It was the hotel logo, printed on the menus and the notepaper too.

A low wall ran all around the building with a ha-ha on the other side and this gave it a sense of imperturbability, as if it had chosen to set itself apart from the real world. On the left, which is to say on the side opposite the drive, a set of discreet, more modern doors opened from the bar onto a very flat, beautifully maintained lawn, and this was where, eight years previously, the wedding lunch had taken place. On the right, set slightly back, were two miniature versions of the main house. One was a chapel and the other a granary that had been converted into a health spa, with a conservatory and indoor swimming pool attached.

Even as I parked the MG on the gravel it occurred to me that any writers wanting to set a murder in a classic country house would find all the material they needed here. And any killers wanting to get rid of a body would have hundreds of acres in which to do it. I wondered if the police had looked for Cecily Traherne in the grounds. She had said she was going for a walk and her car had been found at Woodbridge station, but how could anyone be sure that she had been the one who had driven it?

Before I had even turned off the ignition, a young man appeared and hauled the suitcase out of the boot. He led me into the entrance hall, which was square but gave the illusion of being circular with a round table, a round carpet and a ring of marble pillars supporting a ceiling decorated with a circle of very ornate stucco. Five doors – one of them a modern lift – led in different directions but the man escorted me into a second hallway with a reception desk tucked underneath an impressive stone staircase.

The stairs curved round on themselves and I could see all the way up to the vaulted roof, three floors above. It was almost like being inside a cathedral. A huge window rose up in front of me, some of the panes made of stained glass, although there was nothing religious about it. It was more like something you might find in an old school or even a railway station. Opposite, what I might describe as a landing ran from one side to the other, partly blocked off by a wall but with a semicircular opening cut into it so that if a guest walked past, they would almost certainly be seen from below. The landing connected two corridors that ran the full length of the hotel — the crossbar, if you like, in a large letter H.

A woman in a sharply cut black dress was sitting behind the reception desk, which was made of some dark, polished wood with mirrored edges. It looked out of place. I knew that much of Branlow Hall had been constructed at the start of the eighteenth century and all the other furnishings were deliberately traditional and old-fashioned. A rocking horse stood against the opposite wall, paint peeling and eyes staring. It reminded me of the famous horror story by D. H. Lawrence. There were two small offices behind the reception desk, one on each side. Later, I would learn that Lisa Treherne occupied one and her sister, Cecily, the other. The doors were open and I could see a pair of identical desks with telephones. I wondered if Cecily had made her call to France from here.

'Ms Ryeland?' The receptionist had been expecting me. When she offered me free accommodation, Pauline Treherne had said she would tell the staff I was helping her with a certain matter but not what it was. The girl was around the same age as the man who had met me; in fact, they could have been brother and sister. They were both fair-haired, slightly robotic, possibly Scandinavian.

'Hello!' I placed my handbag between us, ready to provide a credit card if asked.

'I hope you had a good drive from London.'

'Yes, thank you.'

'Mrs Treherne has put you in the Moonflower Wing. You'll be very comfortable there.'

Moonflower. That was the name Alan Conway had given the hotel in his book.

'It's up one flight of stairs or you can take the lift.'

'I think I can manage the stairs, thank you.'

'Lars will take the case for you and show you the room.'

Definitely Scandinavian, then. I followed Lars up the staircase to the first-floor landing. There were oil paintings on the walls – family members from across the centuries, none of them smiling. Lars turned right and we continued behind the opening that I had seen from below. Resting against the wall, I noticed a table with two glass candlesticks and, on a stand between them, a large silver brooch. This was in the shape of a circle with a silver pin and there was a typewritten card, folded in half, describing it as an eighteenth-century figeen, which pleased me as it was a word I had never come across. There was a dog basket with a tartan blanket under the table and I was reminded of Bear, Cecily Treherne's golden retriever.

'Where's the dog?' I asked.

'He went for a walk,' Lars answered vaguely, as if he was surprised I had even asked.

Everything I have described so far was antique but when we reached the corridor, I noticed that electric key-card operators had been fitted to the doors and that we were being watched by a CCTV camera mounted in a corner. It must have been added long after the murder and perhaps as a response to it – otherwise the killer would have been seen. The first door we came to was number ten. Eleven was next door. But what should have been room twelve was blank and there was no room thirteen either, presumably for reasons of superstition. Was it my imagination or had Lars quickened his pace? I could hear the floorboards creaking under his step, the wheels on my suitcase still squeaking as they bumped over the joints.

After room fourteen, we came to a fire door that opened onto a corridor which was obviously new, part of an extension that jutted out towards the rear of the building. It was as if a second, modern hotel had been added to the first and I wondered if it had been like this eight years ago, when Frank Parris had checked in . . . and out. The carpet in the new section had one of those nasty patterns that you would never find in anyone's home. The doors were made out of wood that was both lighter and newer and they were closer together, suggesting smaller rooms on the other side. The lighting was recessed. Was this the Moonflower Wing? I didn't ask Lars, who was well ahead of me, my suitcase still squeaking as it followed him.

I had been given not just a room but a suite at the very end. Lars swiped the key to let us in and I found myself in a bright, comfortable space in various shades of cream and beige with a widescreen TV mounted on the wall. The sheets on the bed were expensive. A complimentary bottle of wine and a bowl of fruit sat, waiting for me, on a table. I went over to the window and looked out at the courtyard behind the hotel and a row of what might have been converted stables on the far side. The health spa with the swimming pool was over to the right. A driveway led up to a large, modern house set back from the hotel. I saw its name, BRANLOW COTTAGE, by the gate.

Lars put my case on one of those folding luggage racks that we would never have had at Polydorus because they took up too much space and also because they were ridiculous.

'Fridge. Air conditioning. Minibar. Coffeemaker ... ' He showed me round the room just in case I couldn't find the way myself. He was polite rather than enthusiastic. 'The Wi-Fi code is on the table and if there is anything you want, you can dial zero for the front desk.'

'Thank you, Lars,' I said.

'Is there anything else you need?'

'Actually, I'd like to go into room twelve. Could I have a key?'

He looked at me peculiarly for a moment but the Trehernes had prepared the way. 'I'll open it for you,' he said.

He went over to the door and there was that nasty moment when I wasn't sure if I should tip him and wondered whether he was expecting it or not. In Crete we had a straw hat in the bar and anyone with any euros to spare threw them in there to be shared out equally among the staff. Generally, I don't like tipping. It feels old-fashioned, a throwback to the days when waiters and hotel staff were seen as belonging to a lower class. Lars didn't agree. He scowled, turned on his heel and left.

I unpacked with a growing sense of discomfort. Transported to an expensive wardrobe in an expensive room, my clothes didn't so much hang as droop. It was a reminder that I'd bought almost nothing new in two years.

Outside, a black Range Rover drove past the stables and into the drive of Branlow Cottage, the wheels crunching on the gravel. I heard the slam of a car door and looked out of the window in time to see a youngish man wearing a padded waistcoat and a cap get out. There was a dog with him. At the same time, the door of the house opened and a young girl with black hair ran towards him, followed by a dark, slim woman carrying a shopping bag. The man scooped the girl up in his arms. I couldn't see much of his face but I knew that he must be Aiden MacNeil. The girl was his daughter, Roxana. The woman must be Eloise, the nanny. He spoke briefly to her and then they turned round and went back into the house.

I felt guilty, as if I had been spying on them. I turned away, snatched up my handbag with money, notepad and cigarettes and left the room, heading back through the fire door to the older part of the hotel and room twelve. It seemed the obvious place to begin. Lars had propped open the door with a wastepaper basket but I didn't want to be disturbed so I removed the basket and the door swung shut behind me.

I found myself in a room that was actually half the size of the one I had been given. There was no bed and no carpet; presumably they had both been taken away, covered in blood. I've read in so many crime books that violent acts leave a sort of echo and I've never quite believed it, but there was definitely an atmosphere in that place . . . in the empty spaces where there should have been furniture, the faded paintwork on the walls showing where pictures had once hung, the curtains that would never be drawn. There were two trolleys heaped up with towels and cleaning equipment, a pile of box-es, an array of machines – toasters, coffeemakers – mops and buckets, all the junk you don't want to see when you check into a smart hotel.

This was where Frank Parris had been killed. I tried to imagine the door opening and someone creeping in. If Frank had been asleep when he was attacked, they would have needed an electronic key card, but then surely Stefan Codres-cu would have had one already. I could tell where the bed must have stood from the position of the electric sockets on either side and I imagined Frank lying in the darkness. On an impulse, I opened the door again. The hinges made no sound but there would have been a buzz or a click as the elec-tric lock disengaged. Would that have been enough to wake him? There had been few details in the newspapers and the Trehernes hadn't been able to add very much more. Some-where there must be a police report that might tell me wheth-er Frank had been standing up or lying down, what he was wearing, exactly when he had died. The storeroom, shabby and decrepit, told me very little.

Standing there, I was suddenly depressed. Why had I left Andreas? What the hell did I think I was doing? If it had been Atticus Pünd coming into Branlow Hall, he'd have solved the crime by now. Perhaps the position of room twelve or the dog basket might have given him a clue. What about the figeen? That was straight out of Agatha Christie, wasn't it?

But I wasn't a detective. I wasn't even an editor any more. I knew nothing.

Lisa Treherne

Pauline and Lawrence Treherne had invited me to join them for supper on the first evening of my stay but when I entered the hotel dining room, Lawrence was sitting on his own. 'I'm afraid Pauline has a headache,' he explained. I noticed that the table was still laid for three. 'Lisa said she would join us,' he added. 'But we're to start without her.'

He looked older than he had in Crete, dressed in a check shirt that hung off him and red corduroy trousers. There were more lines under his eyes and his cheeks had those dark blotches that I've always associated with illness or old age. It was obvious that the disappearance of his daughter was taking its toll and I guessed that the same was true for Pauline, that her 'headache' had been caused by exactly the same thing.

I sat down opposite him. I was wearing a long dress and wedges but I wasn't comfortable. I wanted to kick off my shoes and feel sand beneath my feet.

'It's very good of you to have come, Miss Ryeland,' he began.

'Please ... call me Susan.' I thought we had been through all that.

A waiter came over and we ordered drinks. He had a gin and tonic. I went for a glass of white wine.

'How is your room?' he asked.

'It's very nice, thank you. You have a lovely hotel.'

He sighed. 'It's not really mine any more. My daughters run it now. And it's difficult to take very much pleasure from it at the moment. It was a life's work for Pauline and me, creating the hotel and building it up, but when something like this happens, you have to ask yourself if it was worth it.'

'When did you put in the extension?'

He looked puzzled, as if I had asked something odd.

'Was the hotel like this when Frank Parris was killed?'

'Oh ... yes.' He understood. 'We did the renovation in 2005. We had two new wings added: Moonflower and Barn Owl.' He half smiled. 'The names were Cecily's idea. The moonflower blooms after the sun has gone down and of course the barn owl comes out at night.' He smiled. 'Actually, you may have noticed, we've put owls everywhere.' He picked up the menu and showed me an image stamped in gold on the cover. 'That was Cecily too. She noticed that "barn owl" is an anagram of Branlow and so she had the bright idea to make it our logo.'

I felt my heart sink. Alan Conway had also had a fondness for anagrams. In one of his books, for example, all the characters were jumbled-up versions of London Tube stations. It was a strange game he played with his readers and one that only undermined the quality of his writing.

Lawrence was still talking. 'When we were doing the rebuilding, we added a lift for disabled access,' he explained. 'And we knocked down a wall to enlarge the dining room.'

That was the room we were sitting in. I had reached it from the circular entrance hall and had noticed the new lift on my way in. The kitchen was at the far end, stretching all the way to the back of the hotel. 'Can you get upstairs from the kitchen?' I asked.

'Yes. There's a service lift and a staircase. We put those in at the same time. We also converted the stables into staff quarters and added the swimming pool and the spa.'

I took out my notepad and jotted down what he had just said. What it meant was that whoever had killed Frank Parris could have arrived at room twelve by four separate paths: the lift at the front of the hotel, another at the back, the main staircase and a set of service stairs. If they had already been in the hotel, they could have come down from the second floor. There had been someone on the reception desk all night but it would still have been perfectly easy to get past without being noticed.

But in Crete Pauline Treherne had told me that Stefan Codrescu had been seen entering the room. Why had he been so careless?

'I don't suppose you've had any news,' I said. 'About Cecily.'

Lawrence grimaced. 'The police think she may have been caught on CCTV in Norwich, but that doesn't make a lot of sense. She doesn't know anyone there.'

'Is Detective Superintendent Locke handling the disappearance?'

'Detective Chief Superintendent, you mean. Yes. I can't say I have a lot of faith in him. He was slow getting started – which was actually when it mattered most – and he doesn't seem to be particularly efficient now.' He glanced down gloomily, then asked: 'Have you had a chance to reread the book?'

It was a good question.

You would have thought it would be the first thing I would do – go through the book from cover to cover. But I hadn't even brought it with me. Actually, I didn't have any of Alan's books in Crete: they had too many unpleasant memories. I'd looked into a bookshop while I was in London, meaning to pick up a copy, and had been surprised to find they were out of stock. I could never decide if that was a good or a bad sign when I was in publishing. Great sales or bad distribution?

The truth was that I didn't want to read it yet.

I remembered it well enough: the village of Tawleigh-on-the-Water, the death at Clarence Keep, the various clues, the identity of the killer. I still had my notes somewhere, the email 'discussions' I had with Alan during the editorial process (I've added those inverted commas because he never listened to a word I said). The story held no surprises for me. I knew the plot inside out.

But you have to remember that Alan hid things in the text: not just anagrams, but acrostics, acronyms, words within words. He did it partly to amuse himself but often to indulge the more unpleasant side of his nature. It was already clear to me that he had used many elements of Branlow Hall for *Atticus Pünd Takes the Case*, but what he hadn't done was describe what had actually happened in June 2008. There was no advertising executive, no wedding, no hammer. If Alan, during his brief visit to the hotel, had somehow discovered who had really killed Frank Parris, he could have concealed it in a single word or a name or a description of something completely irrelevant. He could have spelled out the name of the killer in the chapter headings. Something had caught Cecily Treherne's eye when she read the book, but there was very little chance that it would catch mine – not until I knew a great deal more about her and everyone else at the hotel.

'Not yet,' I said, answering Lawrence's question. 'I thought it might be sensible to meet everyone and look round first. I don't know what Alan found when he came here. The more I know about the hotel, the more chance I'll have of making a connection.'

'Yes. That's a good thought.'

'Would it be possible to see the room where Stefan Codrescu was living?'

'I'll take you there after supper. It's being used by one of our other staff members. But I'm sure they won't mind.'

The waiter came over with the drinks and at the same time Lisa Treherne arrived. At least, I assumed it was her. I had seen photographs of her sister, Cecily, in the newspaper: a pretty woman with a rather babyish face, pursed lips, round cheeks. Apart from her fair hair, cut short in an old-fashioned style, this woman looked nothing like her. She was solid, un-smiling, wearing clothes that were deliberately business-like with cheap spectacles and sensible shoes. She had a scar on the side of her mouth and I found it hard to stop myself staring. It was a dead straight line about half an inch long: it could have been cut with a knife. If it had been me I would have softened it with a little concealer but she had allowed it to define her. She was scowling and it was as if she was unable to smile, as if the scar prevented her.

She approached the table like a boxer climbing into the ring and even before she spoke I knew we weren't going to get along. 'So you're Susan Ryeland,' she said. She sat down without any ceremony. 'I'm Lisa Treherne.'

'It's nice to meet you,' I said.

'Is it?'

'Do you want a drink, dear?' Lawrence asked, a little nervously.

'I already told the waiter.' She looked me straight in the eye. 'Was it your idea to send Alan Conway here?'

'I didn't know anything about it,' I told her. 'I knew he was writing the book but I never saw his work until it was finished and I had no idea he had come to this hotel until your father came to see me in Crete.'

I was trying to work out if Lisa was in the book. There is one character in *Atticus Pünd Takes the Case* who has a scar: a beautiful Hollywood actress called Melissa James. Yes. That would have amused Alan, to take this unattractive woman and turn her into the opposite of herself.

Lisa didn't seem to have heard what I'd said. 'Well, if something has happened to Cess because of what was in that book, I hope you'll be pleased with yourself.'

'I really don't think that's fair—' Lawrence began.

But I could stand up for myself. 'Where do you think your sister is?' I asked.

I wondered if Lisa was going to accept that she was dead, destroying any hopes that her father might still have. I could see that for a moment she was tempted, but she couldn't go that far. 'I don't know. When she first went missing, I assumed that she and Ade had had a fight.'

Cess and Ade. The pet names weren't exactly affectionate. They were more a way of saving time.

'Did they argue often?'

'Yes—'

'That's not true,' Lawrence cut in.

'Come on, Dad. I know you like to think of them as the perfect couple. Aiden as the perfect husband, perfect father! But if you ask me, he only ever married Cess because she gave him an easy ride. Golden smile. Blue eyes. But no one ever asks what's going on behind them.'

'What exactly are you saying, Lisa?' I asked. I was surprised she should be so upfront with her feelings.

A second waiter came over with a double whisky on a silver tray. She took it without thanking him.

'I just get fed up with Ade swanning around the hotel as if he runs it. That's all. Especially when I'm the one doing all the heavy lifting.'

'Lisa does the books,' Lawrence explained.

'I do the accounts. Contracts. Insurance, HR and stock control.' She drank half the whisky in one go. 'He schmoozes with the guests.'

'Do you think he killed Frank Parris?' I asked.

Lisa stared at me. I had been deliberately provocative but actually my question was completely logical. If Cecily had been killed, then it was because she knew something about the earlier murder. It followed that whoever killed Frank Parris must have killed her.

'No,' she said, finishing the whisky.

'Why not?'

She looked at me with pity. 'Because it was Stefan! He admitted it. He's in jail.'

A few other guests had begun to drift into the room. It was a quarter to seven, still very light outside. Lawrence picked up one of the menus that had been left on the table. 'Shall we order?' he asked.

I was hungry but I didn't want to interrupt Lisa. I waited for her to continue.

'Hiring Stefan Codrescu was a mistake and we should have fired him right at the start. I said so at the time, although nobody listened to me. He wasn't just a criminal himself. He'd grown up with criminals. We gave him an opportunity and he just sneered at us. He was only here five months, for heaven's sake, but he was ripping us off almost from the moment he walked in.'

'We don't know that,' Lawrence said.

'We do know that, Daddy. I know that.' She turned to me. 'He'd only been here for a few weeks before I started noticing anomalies. I wouldn't imagine you have any idea what it's like, running a hotel, Susan ...'

I could have put her right on that one but I let it pass.

'It's like a machine with a thousand moving parts and the trouble is that if a few of them go missing, nobody notices. The machine doesn't stop. Wine and whisky. Champagne. Fillet steaks. Petty cash. Guests' property: jewellery, watches, designer sunglasses. Linen and towels. Antique furniture. Putting a thief in here is like giving a drug addict the keys to his local Boots.'

52

'When Stefan came here, he'd never been accused of theft,' Lawrence reminded her. But he didn't sound convinced.

'What are you talking about, Daddy? He had been sent to prison for burglary and assault.'

'It's not the same ... '

'You wouldn't listen to me. You never do.' Lisa dismissed him and focused her energies on me. 'I knew something was wrong. Somebody was stealing from us. But whenever I mentioned Stefan's name, everyone ganged up on me.'

'You liked him to start with. You spent lots of time with him.'

'I tried to like him because that was what you all wanted. But the only reason I stayed close to him – and I've told you this enough times – was to see what he was up to. And I was right, wasn't I! What happened in room twelve was horrible, but it showed that I'd been right all along.'

'How much money was actually stolen from Frank Parris's room?' I asked.

'A hundred and fifty pounds,' Lawrence said.

'And you really believe that Stefan would murder someone, hammer them to death, for such a small amount?'

'I'm sure Stefan didn't mean to kill anyone. He sneaked into the room in the middle of the night, thinking he could help himself to whatever and get away with it. But the poor man woke up and challenged him and Stefan lashed out on the spur of the moment.' Lisa sniffed at me. 'It all came out in the trial.'

It didn't make any sense to me. If Stefan hadn't intended to kill Frank Parris, why had he been carrying a hammer? And why go into the room while the occupant was there? But

I didn't say anything. There are some people you just never want to argue with, and Lisa was certainly one of them.

She called the waiter over and ordered another drink. I took the opportunity to order my food. Just a salad and another glass of wine. Lawrence went for a steak.

'Can you tell me what happened on the night of the murder?' I asked and even as I uttered the words I felt slightly ridiculous. They sounded so old-fashioned, so clichéd. If I'd seen them in a novel, I'd have edited them out.

Lawrence took me through it. 'We had thirty friends and relatives staying over the weekend, but as I told you, the hotel was still open to the public and we had paying guests too. Every room was full.

'Frank Parris had checked in two days before the wedding, on the Thursday. He was staying three nights. I remember him because he was quite difficult from the start. He was tired and he was jet-lagged and he didn't like his room so he insisted that we move him.'

'Which room was he in?'

'We'd given him room sixteen. It's in the Moonflower Wing, where you are.'

I had passed room 16 on the way to my suite. It was on the other side of the fire door, where the swirly carpet began.

'He preferred the old part of the hotel,' Lawrence went on. 'Fortunately, we were able to move things around so he got what he wanted. That's very much Aiden's job, incidentally, to keep people happy. And he's very good at it.'

'The person Frank Parris changed with didn't complain?'

'As I recall, he was a retired headmaster, travelling on his own. I don't think he ever knew.'

'Do you remember his name?'

'The headmaster? No. But I can easily find out for you if you like.'

'That would be helpful. Thank you.'

'We had the wedding on the Saturday and we did warn the guests that there would be a certain amount of disruption. For example, we closed the spa early on the Friday evening so that we could give all the staff a drink, outside beside the swimming pool. We wanted them to feel part of the celebration even if they weren't actually coming to the wedding itself. The staff drinks started at eight thirty and finished at ten o'clock.'

'Was Stefan invited?'

'Yes. He was there. So were Aiden and Cecily. Pauline and myself. Lisa ... '

Lisa's plus one, or rather his absence, hung in the air.

'It was a very warm evening. In fact, you may remember that there was quite a heatwave that summer.'

'It was a horrible, hot, sticky night,' Lisa said. 'I couldn't wait to get home.'

'Lisa doesn't live on the estate,' Lawrence said, adding, 'although she could. The grounds extend to almost three hundred acres.'

'Aiden and Cecily have my old place,' Lisa muttered, sourly.

'Branlow Cottage,' I said.

'I moved into Woodbridge, which suits me very well. I left the drinks a long time before ten o'clock. I drove home and went to bed.'

'I'm going to leave Derek to tell you the rest,' Lawrence said. 'He's the night manager and he arrived at about the same time. He wasn't at the party.'

'He wasn't invited?'

'Of course he was invited but Derek doesn't like to socialise. You'll understand when you meet him. He was actually behind reception when the murder took place.'

'When was that?'

'According to the police, Parris was killed around twelve thirty on Friday night.'

'Were you here, Lawrence?'

'No. Pauline and I bought a house in Southwold when we stopped running the hotel. We went home for the night.'

'But we were all there for the wedding the next day,' Lisa said. 'It was such a lovely day ... until, of course, there was a murder. Poor Aiden! I'm sure it wasn't what he was buying into.'

'Really, Lisa, that's too much,' Lawrence protested.

'All I'm saying is that Cess was his meal ticket. What was he doing before he met her? Nothing! He was an estate agent.'

'He was doing very well. And he was a great help to us here at the hotel, whatever you may say,' Lawrence tut-tutted. 'Anyway, I think it's hardly appropriate to talk in this way, given how worried we all are about Cecily.'

'I'm worried about her too!' Lisa exclaimed and to my surprise I saw tears start in her eyes and I knew she was telling the truth. The waiter had arrived with her second whisky and she snatched it off the tray. 'Of course I'm worried about her. She's my sister! And if something's happened to her – that's too horrible to think about.'

She gazed into her drink. The three of us sat in silence.

'What do you remember about the wedding?' I asked.

'It was a wedding like any other. We have weddings here all the time. They're our bread and butter.' She took a breath.

56

'The service was in the rose garden. I was the maid of honour. We had the registrar from Ipswich, then lunch in a marquee on the main lawn. I was sitting next to Aiden's mother who had come down from Glasgow.'

'Was his father there?'

'His father died when Aiden was quite young. Cancer. He has a sister but she wasn't invited. Actually, there was hardly anyone on his side of the family. Mrs MacNeil was quite sweet, a bit of an old lady, very Scottish. I was thinking how boring the whole thing was when I heard screaming coming from somewhere outside the tent and a few minutes later Helen came in, looking like she'd just seen a ghost.'

'Helen?'

'She was head of housekeeping. It turned out that one of the maids had just gone into room twelve and had found Frank Parris with his skull smashed in and bits of brain all over the sheets.' Lisa was almost gloating. Despite what she had said earlier, she couldn't help herself from being amused by the total destruction of her sister's big day. Looking at her, I wondered if she wasn't a little bit unhinged.

'The maid was called Natasha,' Lawrence cut in. 'She'd gone in to clean the room and she discovered the body.'

Lisa downed her whisky in one. 'I don't know what you hope to find, Susan. Stefan admitted to the crime and now he's got what he deserves. It'll be ten years before they even think of letting him out again and serves him right. As for Cess, she'll turn up when it suits her. She likes being the centre of attention. She's probably just playing the drama queen.'

She got unsteadily to her feet and I realised she must have been drinking before she arrived and that the two double whiskies had supplemented many others. 'I'll leave the two of you together,' she said.

'Lisa, you should eat.'

'I'm not hungry.' She leaned towards me. 'You're responsible for Cecily,' she snarled. 'You published the fucking book. You find her.'

Lawrence watched her as she wove her way across the dining room. 'I'm sorry about that,' he said. 'Lisa works very hard. She's actually responsible for the entire running of the hotel. But she can get a bit tired.'

'She doesn't seem to like her sister very much.'

'You shouldn't take any notice of that. Lisa just likes to show off.' He was trying to convince me but he didn't even sound very convinced himself. 'It started when they were very young,' he admitted. 'There was always a lot of rivalry between them.'

'How did she get that scar?'

'Ah, I thought you might ask about that.' He was reluctant to tell me. I waited. 'I'm afraid that was Cecily. It was a complete accident, but ... ' He let out a breath. 'Lisa was twelve and Cecily was ten and they had an argument. Cecily threw a kitchen knife at her. She really didn't mean it to hit her sister. It was just a stupid, childish thing to do when she lost her temper, but the blade absolutely sliced into Lisa and ... well, you've seen the result. Cecily was terribly upset.'

'What were they arguing about?'

'Does it really matter? Boys, probably. They were always jealous of each other's boyfriends. I mean, that's quite common with young girls. Cecily was always the better-looking of the two and if she met someone it would infuriate Lisa.

That's why she's taken against Aiden, incidentally. What she said about him – it's just jealousy. There's absolutely nothing wrong with him, really. He and I have always got along.'

He picked up his wine glass.

'Girls will be girls!'

He said it as a toast but I didn't join in. Girls might be girls, but not, I thought, borderline psychotics. Lisa had been disfigured by Cecily. She had a serious grudge against Aiden. And that grudge, all tied up with some sort of sexual jealousy, might have extended to Stefan Codrescu too.

Serious or murderous?

Which?

The Night Manager

I didn't eat very much dinner. I was stung by what Lisa had said to me and wondered if it was true: I had never unleashed Alan Conway on Branlow Hall but it was undoubtedly true that I had profited by what he had done. Like it or not, I was partly to blame.

After coffee, Lawrence took me out through the kitchen and I noticed the service staircase and the lift leading up to the second floor. We emerged round the back of the hotel and, looking across the courtyard, I saw the driveway that led to Branlow Cottage. There were lights on behind some of the windows. The black Range Rover was still parked outside.

'It's been absolute hell for Aiden,' Lawrence said. 'The moment he reported Cecily missing, he turned himself into the main suspect. It's always the husband in cases like this. But I can't bring myself to believe that he would do anything to hurt my daughter. I've seen them together. I know what they mean to each other.'

'They only have one child?' I said.

'Yes. I was a little sad about that. But it was a difficult birth and I think Cecily just didn't want to go through it all again. Anyway, she was so busy running the hotel.'

'You said that Roxana is seven.' I'd already done the maths. 'When is her birthday?'

Lawrence knew what I was getting at. 'Cecily was already expecting her when she got married – but that wasn't the reason for it. Young people these days don't feel under pressure … not like we did. Aiden's devoted to his daughter. Right now, she's the only thing keeping him sane.'

'Do you think he'll mind talking to me?' It was something that had been worrying me. I was here because I'd been asked to read a book which might or might not be connected to a murder that had taken place eight years before. That was one thing. Interrogating a grieving husband about his missing wife was quite another.

'I'm sure he'll be glad to talk to you. I can ask him if you like.'

'I'd be grateful. Thank you.'

As we talked, we passed the swimming pool which was contained in an oversized conservatory that might have been modelled on Brighton Pavilion. It stood next to a handsome building, a miniature replica of the main house. This had once been a granary store but had been converted into a spa. It was closing for the night and a good-looking young man came out of the side door, dressed in a tracksuit and carrying a sports bag. He noticed us and waved.

'That's Marcus,' Lawrence told me. 'He runs the spa – but he only joined us a couple of years ago.'

'Who was running it when Frank Parris was killed?'

'An Australian. His name was Lionel Corby. But he left soon after. We actually lost quite a few staff, as you might expect.'

'Do you know where he is now?'

'He may have gone back to Australia. I've got his last phone number if that's any help.'

He had come from Australia. So had Frank Parris. It was a connection of sorts. 'Yes. That might be useful,' I said.

We reached the stable block, which had been converted into living quarters for staff: there were five small apartments, studio flats next to each other, each with a door and a single window facing the hotel. A general maintenance room stood at the far end. Lawrence pointed. 'That was where Stefan kept his toolbox, including the hammer that he used for the crime.'

'Can I see?'

I don't know what I expected to find. The room had a concrete floor and several shelves piled up with cardboard boxes, cans of paint, various chemicals ... No lock on the door. Anyone could have come in here. I said so.

'The defence made a lot of that during the trial,' Lawrence agreed. 'Yes, anyone could have taken the hammer. The trouble was, that was the only thing Stefan had on his side and against all the other evidence it was practically meaningless.'

We went to the room next door, which was the one that Stefan had occupied: number five. Lawrence knocked and when there was no answer he took out a Yale key, which he turned in the lock.

'I spoke to Lars earlier,' he explained. 'He's probably at the pub with Inga. They both arrived this year.'

I remembered the smart-looking girl behind the reception desk. 'They're Danish?' I asked.

'Yes. We got them through an agency.' He sighed. 'We don't run our Youth Offender Programme any more.'

The door opened into a perfect shoebox of a room with a single bed beside the door, a desk, a wardrobe and a chest of drawers. A second door led into a corner bathroom with a toilet, sink and shower. I guessed that all five rooms were exactly the same. Lars kept his frighteningly tidy. The bed looked as if it had never been slept in and in the bathroom I could see towels hanging with perfect precision on the rail. Apart from a couple of books on the desk, there was nothing personal in sight at all.

'These Scandinavians are very tidy,' Lawrence muttered, reading my thoughts. 'It certainly wasn't like this when Stefan occupied it.'

That surprised me. 'How do you know?'

'Lionel, the fitness chap I mentioned, used to spend time here. He and Stefan were quite close. You should look at the police reports.'

'That may be easier said than done.'

'I could have a word with DCS Locke.'

'No. It's all right. I know him.' I also knew that there was little chance of Locke sharing anything with me, not even the time of day. I peered into the room, not wanting to step inside. 'They found money in here that belonged to the dead man.'

'Yes. It was under his mattress.'

'Not exactly the most brilliant place to hide stolen cash.'

Lawrence nodded. 'You can think many things about Stefan Codrescu,' he said. 'But one thing is certain. He wasn't too bright.'

'Someone could have planted it.'

'I suppose that's possible, but you have to ask yourself, when? It would have been almost impossible during the day. As you can see, the door faces the hotel and there were dozens of people out here. We had wedding guests, the spa was open, there were security guards, the kitchen staff going back and forth, people looking out of windows. I don't think anyone could have slipped into the room without being seen and believe you me, the police took hundreds of witness statements.

'And it wasn't just the money. They also found traces of blood on the shower floor and on the sheets of Stefan's bed. The forensics people were able to work out that they had been there for more than twelve hours, meaning that they had definitely been there during the night. The narrative was crystal clear. On Friday night, Stefan kills Frank Parris. There's a lot of blood. He comes back and showers and goes to bed and he leaves gigantic footprints the entire way.'

'So if someone did plant the evidence on Stefan, they must have done it sometime after midnight,' I said.

'Yes. But that's not very likely either. First of all, the door self-locks – and before you ask, we did have a duplicate key in Lisa's office. But look at the position of the bed. It's right next to the door. I don't see how anyone could have got in here, messed around with the bed sheets and the shower and then left again without waking Stefan up.'

He closed the door and we walked back to the hotel together.

'Derek should be here by now,' Lawrence said. 'I asked him to come in early to talk to you.' He paused. 'Can I ask you to go easy on him? He's worked at the hotel for ten years and he's a good man. But he's quite fragile. He looks after his mother and she's not at all well. What Alan Conway did to him – to both of them – was actually appalling.'

I remembered that in the book there's a character called Eric Chandler who works as a personal chauffeur and handyman alongside his mother, Phyllis. They appear in the first chapter and it's not a sympathetic portrayal.

'Did he read *Atticus Pünd Takes the Case*?' I asked.

'Fortunately not. Derek doesn't read very much. It might be best not to mention it.'

'I won't.'

'I'll wish you a goodnight, then.'

'Goodnight. Thanks for dinner.'

*

There was absolutely no need for Lawrence Treherne's warning. The moment I saw him, I knew that Derek Endicott was a vulnerable man, eager to please, frightened of giving offence. It was in the blinking eyes behind the spectacles with thick lenses, the hesitant smile, the curly hair that fell haphazardly, without any sense of style. He was in his forties, but his face had a childlike quality, with plump cheeks, thick lips, the sort of skin that suggested he never shaved. He had already taken his place behind the reception desk, tucked away in the cave formed by the staircase that swung diagonally over him on its way up to the first floor. I noticed that he had some food in a plastic Tupperware box as well as a Thermos and a puzzle magazine.

He was expecting me. Lawrence had told him why I was there. He clumsily stood up as I approached, then sat down before he had become fully vertical. It was quite cool in the reception area, but I noticed a sheen of sweat on his neck and on the sides of his face.

'Mr Endicott ... ' I began.

'Derek. Please. That's what everyone calls me.' He had a wheezy, high-pitched voice.

'You know why I'm here?'

'Yes. Mr Treherne asked me to come in early tonight.'

He waited nervously for the first question and I tried to put him at ease. 'You were here on the night Mr Parris was killed. What you saw or heard could be tremendously helpful.'

He frowned. 'I thought you were here because of Cecily.'

'Well, it's possible the two are connected.'

He thought about that for a moment. I could actually see the mental process in his eyes. 'Yes. You could be right.'

I leaned against the desk. 'I know it was a long time ago, but I wonder if you can remember what happened that night?'

'Of course I can remember! It was terrible. I didn't meet Mr Parris. I don't really see any of the guests unless they put me on the day shift and they only do that when they're short-staffed. Actually, I did see Mr Parris go upstairs. It was after dinner, but we didn't speak.' He corrected himself a second time. 'No. That's not true. We spoke on the phone. On Thursday. He called down from his room. He wanted to order a taxi first thing Friday morning. I did that for him.'

'Where did he want to go?'

'Heath House in Westleton. I wrote it down in the book. That was how I was able to remember when the police asked me, and anyway I know that house. It's very close to where I live with my mum. I hated having the police here. This is such a beautiful hotel. People come here to rest and to relax. Not for ... '

He couldn't work out a way to finish the sentence and fell silent.

'To be honest with you, I wasn't feeling very well that night, the night before the wedding,' he went on, eventually. 'I was upset ... '

'What had upset you?'

'No. I mean ... my stomach was upset. It was something I'd eaten.'

'You didn't go to the party.'

'No. But I was invited! I was so happy for Cecily and for Mr MacNeil.' It was interesting that Cecily seemed to be the only person in the hotel he referred to by their first name. 'I thought they were a perfect match. And it was lovely to see her so happy. Do you know where she is?'

'I'm hoping to find out.'

'I hope nothing's happened to her. She's one of the kindest people. Nothing is ever too much trouble. She's always been very good to me.'

'Can you tell me what happened on the night Mr Parris was killed?' I asked.

'Not really.' Despite his protestation, Derek had surely rehearsed all this. He drew a breath then plunged in. 'I was behind my desk – here – at ten o'clock. That was about the time the staff party finished. Everyone sounded as if they'd had a good time. They were all very happy.

'Mr Parris went up to his room about five minutes after I arrived, so that would have been about five past ten. After that, I saw quite a few of the guests go past; some of them were members of the public and some of them were here for the wedding. But anyway, at midnight I was on my own – which is fine. I like this job because I don't mind being by myself. Mother makes me a sandwich and I've got something to read and sometimes I listen to the radio. Cecily said I should watch films on the computer but I don't like to do that because I think it's my job to stay alert.'

'So did you hear or see anything that night?'

'I'm just coming to that!' He took another breath. 'A little bit after midnight, Bear suddenly cried out.'

'Bear? The dog?'

'Cecily's dog. Most of the time he sleeps in the house but sometimes he spends the night over here on the first floor and that was where he was, in his basket.' Derek pointed up towards the circular opening, the gallery on the first floor. It was impossible to see the basket from where he was sitting, but any sound would have carried down. 'They didn't want him with them because of the wedding and everything else going on,' he continued, 'so he'd gone to bed up there.'

'And he cried out.'

'I thought someone must have stepped on his tail or something so I went up the stairs. But there was no one there. Bear was lying in his basket, absolutely fine. He must have just had a bad dream. I knelt down and gave him a stroke and it was while I was there that someone went past.'

'Went past where?'

'Along the corridor. Going from the new lift towards Moonflower Wing.'

I've already described Branlow Hall as being built in the shape of a letter H. When Derek was crouching beside the dog, he would have been about midway along the cross-bar with a corridor at each end. Whoever had travelled towards room twelve must have come from the front of the building.

'Could they have come from outside the hotel?' I asked.

'I don't know.'

'But the front door. Was it locked?'

Derek shook his head. 'We never locked the doors. Not in those days. There wasn't any need.' He grimaced and added portentously: 'We do now.'

'And you didn't see who it was.' I almost had no need to ask. The figure, flitting along the corridor, would have been in his line of vision for less than a second.

'I thought it was Stefan,' Derek admitted. The next words tumbled out quickly, in anguish. 'I didn't want to get anyone into trouble. I only told the police what I saw. He was carrying a toolbox. It was Stefan's toolbox. I'd seen it lots of times. And he was wearing a knitted hat.' He put his hands on his head to show me what he meant.

'You mean ... a beanie?'

'Yes. Stefan often wore a beanie. But the lights were on low and it was so quick. I told the police I couldn't be sure.'

69

'So what did you do next?' I asked. 'After you saw the man with the toolbox?'

'I went to the main corridor to see who it was – but by the time I got there it was too late. He'd gone.'

'He'd gone into one of the rooms.'

'He must have.' Derek looked miserable, as if the whole thing was somehow his fault. 'The police said he'd gone into room twelve.'

Room twelve was only five or six paces away from the point where the landing met the corridor and it was on the near side of the fire door. If Derek had walked forward straight away, the intruder must have disappeared in a matter of seconds.

'Did you hear him knock?'

'No.'

'Did anyone say anything?'

'No.'

'So what did you think?'

'I didn't think anything. I mean, I thought maybe Stefan had gone into one of the rooms to mend something – a toilet or something – although that didn't make any sense because if anyone had needed him they'd have had to call me. But everything was quiet. There wasn't any noise or anything. So after a bit I just went back to my desk and that was the end of it.'

'You didn't hear anything else?'

'No.' He shook his head.

'Derek ... ' How could I put this gently? 'Frank Parris was attacked with a hammer. He must have cried out. I can't believe you didn't hear him.'

'I didn't hear anything!' His voice rose. 'I was all the way back downstairs and I was listening to music on the radio ...'

'All right.' I waited for him to calm down. 'Who discovered the body?' I asked.

'That was Natasha. She was one of the maids. I think she was Russian or something.' His eyes widened as he remembered what had happened. 'She found it when she went in to clean the room. They say she screamed and screamed.'

'But that wasn't until much later ... the next day.'

'Yes.' Derek leaned forward and almost whispered, 'Someone had put a "Do Not Disturb" sign on the door of number twelve!' he told me. 'They did it on purpose. So no one would know.'

'So why did Natasha go in, then?'

'Because someone took it off again.'

'Who took it off?'

'I don't know. They never found out.'

He had nothing more to say. I could see that. He looked exhausted.

'Thank you, Derek,' I said.

'I wish it had never happened. The hotel has never been the same since then. There's always been an atmosphere ... I've said it often enough to my mum. It's as if there's something evil here. And now Cecily going missing. I knew something was wrong when she made that phone call. She was so upset. It's all part of the same thing and I don't think it's ever going to end.'

'Do you have any idea who killed Frank Parris?'

He was surprised by my question, as if nobody had ever asked him what he thought. 'It wasn't Stefan,' he said. 'Even if it was Stefan I saw going along the corridor, I'm sure it wasn't him. He seemed such a nice sort of guy. He was very quiet. I know Miss Treherne – Lisa, I mean – didn't like him very much and she said he was dishonest, but he seemed all right to me. Do you think they'll find her?'

'Cecily Treherne?'

'Yes.'

'I'm sure they will. I'm sure she'll turn up safe and sound.'

That was what I said, but in my heart I knew I was lying. I hadn't even been in the hotel for one full day but something there had reached out to me. Maybe it was the sense of evil that Derek had been talking about. But I was quite sure that Cecily was already dead.

Face Time

Was I getting old?

I was examining myself on the computer screen as I tried to connect with Crete and although it's true that the camera on a MacBook Air never does anyone any favours, I wasn't too happy with what I saw. I looked tired. Two years of Cretan sun and cigarette smoke had not done great things for my skin. After I'd left London I'd stopped putting any colour in my hair and I wasn't sure if the result was delightfully natural or plain drab. I've never been very fashion-conscious. Kicking around alone in my flat in Crouch End, I used to go for oversized T-shirts and leggings. Of course I'd dress up for work, but with forced retirement I'd found myself liberated from the three S's – suits, stockings and stilettos – and in the Greek sunshine I'd dressed in anything that was light and loose-fitting. Andreas had always said that he loved me as I was and that there was no need to impress him, but looking at myself, I wondered if I wasn't letting myself go – a horrible phrase that brought to mind debauchery and decay.

There was a zing and my image was pushed into the corner where it belonged and in its place Andreas's face filled the screen. I had been afraid that he would be out or – worse – that he would be in and wouldn't answer. But there he was, sitting on our terrace. As he leaned back, I could see the shutters behind him and the tubs full of sage and oregano that I had planted myself. His computer was on the glass table with the crack in it, the one we had said we must replace but never would.

'*Yassou, agapiti mou!*' he said. It was a joke between us that every morning, from the first day I had arrived at the hotel, he would greet me in Greek, but I wondered now if he wasn't taunting me, reminding me that I was so far away from him.

'How are you?' I asked.

'I'm missing you.'

'How's the hotel?'

'The hotel . . . is the hotel! It's still here.'

Andreas's face lit up my screen – and I mean that in every sense. His dark skin and thick black hair emphasised the dazzling white of his teeth and I could actually see the sparkle in his eyes. He was an incredibly handsome man and looking at him in front of me, I felt a longing to climb through that rectangular window and throw myself into his arms. I hadn't left him. That was what I told myself. I had just gone away for a week. I would go back to Crete when this was all over, ten thousand pounds richer. In the end, the whole experience would bring us closer together.

'Where are you now?' Andreas asked.

'At the hotel. Branlow Hall.'

'What's it like?'

'It's barking mad. There are oil paintings on the walls and stained-glass windows. Some of the rooms have four-poster beds. You'd love it.'

'Who are you sharing yours with?'

'Stop it!'

'I miss having you in mine. It's not the same here without you. Lots of the regulars have complained.'

The mood had changed and we were serious. I realised now that I had left Crete without even thinking about the immediate consequences. There had been no discussion between us, no attempt to iron out the difficulties that had insinuated themselves into our relationship. Our last conversation had been acrimonious. *I don't want you to go,* he had said. But I had gone anyway. I wondered now if I had behaved badly and, worse still, if I had broken something that was precious to me.

'How are Panos and Vangelis?' I asked.

'They're fine.'

'Don't they miss me?'

'Of course they miss you.' He spread his hands so that they disappeared on either side of the screen. 'But we get by.'

I scowled. 'You mean, you can manage without me.'

'We need the money! Have you got it yet?'

In fact, Lawrence hadn't paid me anything so far. 'I'm chasing it,' I said.

'If it hadn't been for the money, I wouldn't have let you go.'

He sounded so Greek when he said that. I couldn't tell if he was joking or not.

'So tell me about the murder,' he went on. 'Do you know who did it?'

'I don't know anything yet.'

'It was the husband.'

'What?'

'The woman who disappeared. Of course he did it. It's always the husband.'

'I haven't even spoken to him yet. And it's more complicated than that. This is all about something that happened eight years ago. If someone has killed Cecily, it was because of that.'

Andreas pointed at the screen. His finger loomed towards me, out of perspective. 'Just you take care of yourself. Remember, if you get into trouble, I won't be there to help you.'

'Why don't you get on a plane?' I said, wanting him beside me.

'The Polydorus can manage without you. But it can't manage without both of us.'

I heard shouting. It was coming from underneath the terrace, I think, but it was impossible to tell who it was. Andreas listened, then shrugged his shoulders in a gesture of regret. 'I have to go,' he said.

'If it's the microwave, just turn it off and then on again.'

'That's true of everything in the hotel. In the whole country!' He leaned forward. 'I miss you, Susan. And I worry about you. Don't put yourself in any danger.'

'I won't.'

The shouting continued, louder.

'I love you.'

'I love you.'

Two thousand miles apart, we reached towards each other. Our fingers found the cursor at the same moment. We pressed. The screen went blank.

Heath House, Westleton

The next morning began with an unpleasant surprise.

I'd had breakfast in my room and was just on my way downstairs when a man in a suit appeared, walking briskly from the front of the hotel towards reception. I recognised him at once: those angry eyes, his black skin, his muscular neck and shoulders, even the way he walked – as if searching for a wall to bulldoze his way through. With or without his promotion, there could be no mistaking Detective Chief Superintendent Richard Locke and I briefly considered turning round and going back to my room as if I had forgotten something rather than risk running into him a second time. He had been angry enough when I had involved myself in his last investigation.

But I was already committed. I couldn't avoid him. So I kept my head down and hurried forward, pretending not to notice him, as if lost in my own thoughts. We passed within inches of each other at the foot of the stairs and although he must have seen me, he didn't actually recognise me, which I couldn't help feeling showed a distinct lack of observational skills in someone who called himself a detective. To be fair, his mind must have been on other things. I heard him ask for Aiden MacNeil and realised he had come to report on the search for his wife and, presumably, his lack of progress. I was glad that Locke hadn't seen me. It was a distraction that neither of us needed.

It also gave me an excuse to postpone seeing Aiden myself, which was a meeting I was still dreading. I didn't agree with what Andreas had said. Just because Aiden was married to Cecily, it didn't make him the prime suspect in her disappearance. On the contrary, and ignoring what Lisa had said, all the evidence suggested that the two of them had been happy together. They also had a child. Surely that made it less likely that he would want to do her harm?

It was a relief to climb into my dear old MG Roadster and to feel the rush as it carried me away from the hotel. It was a beautiful day but I wanted to get on the road as quickly as possible and waited until I got to the end of the drive before stopping and folding down the roof. After that, I continued on my way, pushing against the speed limit, feeling the wind streaming over my shoulders and tangling my hair. I spun through green leaves and woodland until I reached the A12, then headed north to Westleton. Frank Parris had visited somewhere called Heath House on the day he was killed. I wondered if this was where his relatives had lived and, more to the point, if they were still there.

Westleton is a funny village in that it isn't really a village at all, more a confluence of roads. There's the Yoxford Road to Yoxford, the Dunwich Road to Dunwich and the Blythburgh Road to Blythburgh, but there doesn't seem to be a Westleton

Road to Westleton. It's as if someone is trying to tell you that there's no particular reason to visit the place where you actually are. It has an old-fashioned garage, a pub that's sign-posted but nowhere to be seen, a second-hand bookshop and not much else. That said, it's on the edge of a superb nature reserve and you can walk to the sea. I'm sure it's a lovely place to live.

Heath House wasn't easy to find, especially in an old car without satnav. I had printed up a map at the hotel but drove in circles until I came across a farmer hosing down a tractor: he directed me to a narrow lane I hadn't noticed, mainly because it had no name. The lane led me away from the centre of the village and into the nature reserve itself, finally petering out on a stretch of grassland with a timber-frame farmhouse on the other side. This was Heath House. The name was written on an American-style mailbox beside the gate.

It was the sort of home designed to be seen on a summer morning with the lawns freshly mown, the flowers in full bloom, the hammock swaying beneath the trees and so on. It must have been a hundred years old and even without going in I knew there would be exposed beams and open fireplaces, comfy nooks and ceilings where you would have to be careful not to bang your head. It wasn't particularly beautiful: the roof had been badly repaired with tiles that changed colour halfway across, and an ugly modern conservatory had been added to one side. But it was a house that was completely comfortable with itself. It must have had five or six bedrooms, two of them tucked up in the eaves. A set of wind chimes hung from a tree, tinkling meditatively in the breeze.

I parked the car and got out. There was no need to lock it or to close the roof. As I opened the gate, I noticed a man in dark blue overalls painting a window frame. He was short and thin, quite pale, with close-cropped hair and round glasses. Did he own the house? Or did he work for the man who owned the house? It was hard to be sure.

'Hello,' he said. He didn't seem at all surprised to see me. He was smiling.

'Do you live here?' I asked.

'Yes. How can I help you?'

I hadn't been prepared for such conviviality and I wasn't sure how to introduce myself. 'I'm very sorry to bust in on you like this,' I said, 'but I wondered if I could have a word.' He waited for more. 'It's about Branlow Hall.'

At once he was interested. 'Oh yes?'

'I'm staying there.'

'Lucky you. It's a nice hotel.'

'I'm asking questions about something that happened quite a long time ago. Did you by any chance know a man called Frank Parris?'

'Yes. I knew Frank.' He noticed he was still holding the paintbrush and put it down. 'Why don't you come in and have a cup of tea?'

It baffled me that he was so amiable. He seemed not just willing but eager to talk to me. 'Thank you,' I said. I held out a hand. 'I'm Susan Ryeland.'

He examined his own hand, which was smudged with white paint. 'Martin Williams. Forgive me if I don't shake hands. Come this way . . . '

He led me round the side and in through a sliding door. The interior of the house was exactly as I had imagined it. The kitchen was large and homely, with an Aga, an island for food preparation, pots hanging from the rafters and a pine kitchen table with eight chairs. It had modern windows looking out onto the garden and an archway leading into a hallway with red-brick walls, a round, antique table and a staircase leading up. The family did its shopping at Waitrose. There were two Bags for Life on the floor next to a row of wellington boots, a cat's litter tray, an ironing board, tennis rackets, a laundry basket and a bicycle pump. The house wasn't untidy so much as lived in. Everything was where it was meant to be. Ordnance Survey maps and birdwatching books lay spread out on the table, along with a copy of the *Guardian*. There were framed photographs everywhere – two girls from infancy to their early twenties.

'Builder's or peppermint?' Martin asked, flicking on the kettle.

But before I could answer, a woman came into the room. She was a little shorter than him, about the same age – as a couple, they were in perfect proportion. She reminded me a little of Lisa Treherne: she had that same angry quality. The difference was that she was more defensive. This was her territory and she didn't want me here.

'This is Joanne,' Martin said. He turned to her. 'And this is Susan. She's come over from Branlow Hall.'

'Branlow Hall?'

'Yes. She wants to know about Frank.'

Joanne's face changed when she heard that. She had been vaguely unwelcoming a minute or so ago but now she looked offended. She might even have been afraid.

'It's quite difficult to explain . . . ' I began, trying to put her at ease.

Next to the Aga, the electric kettle began to hiss. 'I was just making Susan some tea,' Martin said. 'What will it be?'

'Builder's would be fine,' I said.

'I'll do it.' Joanne reached for mugs and tea bags.

'No, no, darling. You sit down and look after our guest.' He smiled at me. 'We don't get many visitors out this way. It's always nice to have company.'

Why did I get the impression that the two of them were playing some sort of game? They reminded me of the husband and wife in *Who's Afraid of Virginia Woolf?*, the ones who invite a young couple into their home only to rip them apart.

Joanne and I sat down at the table and I asked her about Westleton while Martin made the tea. I forget what she told me. I just remember the way she stared at me, so combative and intense. I was glad when Martin joined us. Unlike her, he was completely relaxed. He'd even brought a plate of biscuits.

'So why are you interested in Frank?' he asked.

'Were you related to him?' I asked him back.

'Yes.' Martin was completely unfazed. 'He was my brother-in-law. Joanne's his sister.'

'And he'd come to Suffolk to see you.'

'Forgive me, Susan, but you haven't answered my original question.' He smiled at me. 'Why are you asking questions about him?'

I nodded. 'I'm sure you've heard that Cecily Treherne has disappeared. Her parents own the hotel.'

'Yes. We read about that in the papers.'

'They asked me to help them because they think that her disappearance may be connected to Frank's death.'

'What are you? A clairvoyant or something?'

'No. I used to work in publishing. One of my authors wrote about what happened and they think there may be a connection.' It was too difficult to explain everything so I dived straight in. 'Did you see Frank the weekend he died?'

For a moment, I thought they might deny it. Joanne seemed to flinch but Martin didn't even hesitate. 'Oh yes. He came round here the same day it happened. He was killed on a Friday night if I remember correctly. And he came here that same morning, just after breakfast. What time was it, darling?'

'About ten o'clock,' Joanne answered, still staring at me.

'Can you tell me why?'

'He'd just come back from Australia. He wanted to see us.'

'He didn't stay with you.'

'No. We'd have been happy to have put him up but he didn't even let us know he was in the country until he called from the hotel. That was Frank for you. He was full of surprises.'

I didn't believe a single word he was saying to me and the strange thing was, I don't think he wanted me to. Everything he said, even that playful smile of his ... it was all a performance. He was like a magician daring me to pick a card in the certain knowledge that in two seconds' time it would have changed into a different one. It was a very strange way to behave considering I was talking about a man, a family member, who had been brutally killed.

I turned to Joanne. I thought it might be easier getting through to her. 'Look, I hate intruding,' I said. 'I know it's none of my business, but as I explained, I'm just trying to find Cecily and anything you can tell me about what happened that weekend might help.'

'I don't think we have anything to say—' Joanne began.

'You can ask anything you like,' Martin cut in. 'We've got nothing to hide.'

In Alan Conway's novels, people only said that when they most definitely did have something to hide.

I looked around me. 'How long have you been here?' I asked. I was deliberately changing the subject, coming in from a different angle.

'We moved in around . . . ' Martin counted it out on his fingers. 'Well, it must have been seven years before Frank went to Australia – 1998. It was the year Joanne's mother died.'

'This was her house?'

'Yes. We were living in London before that. I was working for an insurance broker in the city. Guest Krieger . . . I don't suppose you'll have heard of them. They specialise in art.'

'I don't have any art.'

'Well, fortunately there are plenty of wealthy clients who do.' He flashed that strange smile of his. It was beginning to annoy me. 'Joanne had always wanted to move out of London and as it happens, most of my work is done over the telephone. It doesn't matter where I am. Our girls were just about to start school when this house became available and so we moved in.'

'Where were your girls at school?' I asked.

'Woodbridge School.'

'My sister sent her children there,' I told them. 'My partner used to teach there.'

'It did very well for them,' Joanne said, loosening just a little. 'They're at university now.'

'They must have been pleased to see their uncle.'

'They didn't see him. They weren't at home when he visited.'

'And he didn't want to meet them? After he'd come all the way from Australia?'

'Frank was here on business,' Martin said, allowing just a little impatience to creep into his voice. He had been holding a biscuit and now he snapped it in half and laid both pieces down. 'It's very sad but he'd lost a lot of money setting up his Australian business. He came back to England with almost nothing. He had this idea of starting another agency and he wanted us to invest.' He shook his head. 'I'm afraid it was out of the question. I work for myself now and I do well enough out of it, but there was no way I was going into business with him. It wouldn't have worked.'

'Because … ?'

'Because I didn't like him. Neither of us did.'

And there it was, suddenly out there. An admission of sorts. But where exactly did it lead?

Joanne set down her cup and saucer, the one rattling against the other. 'It wasn't really a question of liking him or disliking him,' she said. 'Frank and I had very little in common. To start with, there was the age difference. But we'd also made some very different life choices. When I was in London, I worked as a payment administrator with the NHS. I had Martin and the children. I'm not saying I disapproved, but Frank had a lifestyle that was completely alien to me.'

'In what way?'

'Well, there was his sexuality, of course. He was gay and I've got nothing against that. But why did he have to shove it in your face? There were always parties and drugs and those clothes he used to wear and so many young men—'

'Steady on!' Martin seemed amused by his wife's indignation. He tapped her gently on the arm. 'Better watch out for the PC brigade!'

'You know what I thought of him, Martin. I just thought it was disgusting, that's all.'

'Frank liked to show off,' Martin said. 'That's all.'

'So what happened when he came here?' I asked.

'He told us that he'd lost a lot of money.' Martin had taken over again. 'He wanted us to help him. We said we'd think about it, although we'd both made up our minds that it wasn't going to happen. We called him a taxi and he went back to the hotel.'

'Did he mention the wedding?'

'As a matter of fact, he was quite pissed off about it. The place was jammed and there was a big marquee in the garden which spoiled the view. He said they should have given him a discount.'

'Did he say anything about Cecily? Or her fiancé, Aiden MacNeil?'

'He didn't mention either of them. I wish I could tell you more, Susan. But he was only here for about forty-five minutes. We had tea. We talked. And then he left.'

Joanne clearly wanted me to do the same. I had finished my tea and no second cup was being offered. I got to my feet. 'You've both been very kind,' I said. 'I may be in Suffolk for a few more days. Do you mind if I come back?'

'You're welcome any time,' Martin said. 'If you have any more questions we'll be happy to answer them, won't we, Jo?'

'Let me show you out.' Joanne had got up too. She gestured towards the archway.

If she had been just a little less formal, she might have escorted me through the sliding doors, the way I had come in. But she clearly felt a need to take me through the hallway and out through the front door, which was how I came to see the cork board half concealed behind the Aga and, as we walked past, the business card pinned in the corner.

Wesley & Khan – Solicitors
Framlingham

It was Sajid Khan who had told Lawrence and Pauline Treherne where they could find me. He had once represented Alan Conway. In what way, I wondered, was he connected to Martin and Joanne Williams?

I was about to ask Joanne how she knew him but I never got the chance. She had been tight-lipped as she led me out of the kitchen but suddenly she turned round and I saw that something extraordinary had happened. She was furious. She was staring at me as if she wanted to kill me.

'I don't want you to come here again,' she hissed, keeping her voice low so that Martin wouldn't hear.

'I'm sorry?'

'Just go away. We never wanted to see Frank and we don't want to see you. Whatever's happened at the hotel, it's got nothing to do with us. So piss off and leave us alone.'

I don't even remember stepping out of the house. I just remember the door slamming behind me and being left with the knowledge that I had no idea what had just happened, but whatever it was, it made no sense at all.

Branlow Cottage

There was no one around when I got back to the hotel and no sign of any police car, which made me think (and hope) that Detective Chief Superintendent Locke must have left. It was just before midday, which seemed like a good time to call on Aiden MacNeil. I still had a certain dread of meeting him but knew I couldn't put it off any longer. I phoned Lawrence from the car, but it was Pauline who answered.

'Lawrence is in the garden,' she said. 'I'm sorry I couldn't see you yesterday. I wasn't feeling very well.'

'That's all right, Pauline. I'm just on my way to see Aiden.'

'Oh yes. He talked to the police this morning.'

'Is there any news?'

'Nothing.'

'I was just wondering if Lawrence spoke to him. He said he was going to mention that I might call in.'

'I don't know. Hold on a moment. I'll ask him.'

There was a click as she put the phone down and then, in the distance, her voice calling through the window: 'Daaaahling?' I waited about a minute and then she came back, slightly breathless. 'Yes. He's waiting to hear from you.'

'He doesn't mind?'

'Not at all. Anything that might help find Cecily ...'

That reassured me.

I walked through the hotel, passing Lars, who was sitting behind the reception desk reading a Danish football magazine called *Tipsbladet*. He didn't look up as I went past. I continued out the back, past the spa and swimming pool and along the gravel drive that led to Branlow Cottage.

Why were they pretending it was a cottage? What they had built was a solid, three-storey house standing in its own grounds, surrounded by a low wall and a gate. There was a swing in the garden and a partly deflated paddling pool. The Range Rover was parked in the drive. Walking past it with my feet crunching on the gravel, I had the strangest feeling of trepidation, even of fear. But I wasn't afraid of Aiden. I was thinking of Cecily, a daughter and a wife and a mother of a seven-year-old girl. She had gone for a walk in the Suffolk countryside and had never come back. Was there anything worse that could happen to anyone? When you live in the country, you spend every minute of the day surrounded by a vast emptiness. I could feel it now. But you never think for a minute that you might become part of it.

As I approached the front door it opened and Aiden came out, walking towards me. He had seen me from the window. He held out a hand. 'You must be Susan Ryeland.'

'Yes.'

'It's good timing. Roxie's out with Eloise. She's off school at the moment. Come on in.'

My first impressions of Aiden surprised me. He was a very handsome man, fair-haired, blue-eyed, in great shape. He was wearing a polo shirt, jeans and loafers. From what the Trehernes had told me, I knew he was thirty-two years old but he looked at least five years younger, with a Peter Pan quality that expressed itself even in the way he moved, light on his feet. I followed him into the kitchen and, without asking me, he flicked on the kettle. The house was very clean and orderly. There was nothing out of place on any of the surfaces.

'When did you arrive?' he asked. It was only when he turned round that I saw the tiredness in his eyes, the worry lines. He hadn't been sleeping properly. He'd lost weight.

'Yesterday.' I didn't know how to begin. 'I'm very sorry,' I said. 'This must be awful for you.'

'Awful?' He half smiled as he considered the word. 'That doesn't even begin to describe it, if you want the truth, Susan. What's awful is that the fucking police think I had something to do with it. What's awful is that they've been here seven or eight times and they still don't have a fucking clue.'

There was a ragged quality to his voice. It was as if he was speaking with a bad sore throat.

'I know Detective Chief Superintendent Locke,' I said. 'He's a very thorough man.'

'Do you think so? If Detective Locke and his friends had been a bit more thorough to begin with, Cecily might have been home by now.'

I watched him make the tea. He did it with exactly the same taut, jerky movements that an alcoholic might use to pour himself a glass of Scotch and he talked all the while, even with his back to me.

'I called the police at eight o'clock on the evening she disappeared. That was a Wednesday. She should have been back at six to help put Roxana to bed and I rang her mobile a dozen times. No answer. I knew something was wrong but it was another hour before someone turned up – a pair of "community officers" – and even then they didn't take it ser-iously. Had we had an argument? Had she been depressed? It was only when the dog showed up at Woodbridge station two hours later that they began to take action. Her car was there too.'

'The Range Rover?'

'No. That's mine. She drives a Golf Estate.'

I noticed the present tense. Aiden hadn't hesitated. He thought she was still alive.

'What did Locke tell you today?' I asked.

'He told me nothing – which is exactly how much pro-gress they've made.' He reached into the fridge and took out a carton of milk. He slammed it down on the counter, al-most crumpling it. 'You have no idea what it's been like,' he said. 'They've taken her bank details, her medical records, photographs – there was one of us on our wedding day that was in all the newspapers. They had a hundred people searching around the River Deben. Nothing. And then we had reports. She'd been seen in London. She was in Nor-wich. She was in Amsterdam – although how she managed that when her passport was still upstairs, I don't know.'

He poured the milk.

'I'm told that the first seventy-two hours are the ones that matter. People who were in the area are still there and they may remember things. You can still find evidence. Did you know that eighty per cent of all people who disappear are found forty kilometres from where they live?'

'I didn't know that.'

'Locke told me. He thought it would cheer me up. But they haven't found her and it's been over a week now.'

He brought the tea over and we sat facing each other, neither of us touching it. I wanted a cigarette but I knew Aiden didn't smoke. There was no smell in the house and his teeth were too white. I thought of what Andreas had said on Face-Time. *'Of course he did it. It's always the husband.'* Well, either Aiden MacNeil was the most brilliant actor I'd ever met or he was on the edge of a breakdown. I looked at him sitting hunched up opposite me. There wasn't a single part of him that was relaxed. He was a man torn apart.

'Your parents-in-law think that Cecily's disappearance may have something to do with a book she read,' I began.

He nodded. *'Atticus Pünd Takes the Case.* Yes. They told me.'

'Have you read it?'

'Yes.' There was a long pause. 'I was the one who gave it to her. I told her to read it.' Suddenly he was angry. 'If it's true, if she's disappeared because of something in that book, then it's my fault. I wish I'd never heard of the bloody thing.'

'How did you hear of it?'

'One of the guests mentioned it to me. That's my job here, really. I talk to the guests. I keep them happy. Cecily manages everything and Lisa does the finances. I'm just PR.' He got up and went over to a sideboard, talking as he went. 'I met Alan Conway when he came here all those years ago but I had no idea that he was going to write a book about us. In fact, he told me quite specifically that he wouldn't ... the bastard. Then this guest started talking about it and said there was a hotel in the book called the Moonflower and of course we have a wing here with the same name. So I went out and got a copy and of course I saw at once that we were all in it. Lawrence and Pauline, Derek – the night manager – me ... '

He turned round and now he was holding a brand-new paperback copy. I recognised the cover with its silhouette of Atticus Pünd, the title in raised letters, 'THE *SUNDAY TIMES* BESTSELLER' printed proudly at the top. How many hours had I spent working on the look of the series? I remembered talking it through with production, telling them how we had to avoid the simple outlines and the pastel colours of a long-forgotten Enid Blyton England even if that was where these books were effectively set. There were plenty of publishers – the British Library Crime Classics, for example – who were already crowding out the front table at Waterstones with their vintage editions and we had to stand apart from them. Alan was an original, modern author, much more than an imitator of Dorothy L. Sayers or John Dickson Carr. That was the message I wanted to get across. After Alan died, when Orion Books bought the series, they'd rejacketed but they hadn't changed the design. It was still, largely, my work.

'Cecily read it. Did she say anything to you?'

'Very briefly. She said there was something strange about it and that it made her think maybe Stefan hadn't done it after all. The murder, I mean. But that's all she said to me, Susan. I would have asked her what she was going on about but we had issues at the hotel. Roxana wasn't sleeping. Lisa was being even more of a bitch than usual. There were all sorts of things happening and we just didn't have time to sit down and talk.'

We both sat staring at the tea, realising at the same time that we didn't want it. He got up and took a bottle of wine out of the fridge. He poured two glasses. 'I'm trying to hold it all together for Roxana,' he said. 'She doesn't really understand what's happening except that Mummy's gone away. How am I meant to explain this to her?' He took a gulp of wine.

I gave him a few moments for the alcohol to take its effect. Then I asked: 'Do you mind talking about the wedding? About you and Cecily?'

'Of course not. If it will help.'

'How did the two of you meet?'

'She'd come down to London because she was thinking about buying a flat. I'm actually from Glasgow myself. I was living there with my mum.'

'She came to the wedding.'

'Yes.'

'She hasn't come down now – to help?'

He shook his head. 'She has Alzheimer's. My sister, Jodie, looks after her. But I wouldn't want them here anyway. I've got Eloise. There's nothing they can do.'

'I'm sorry,' I said. 'Go on.'

'I moved south ... in about 2001, I think it was. I got a job as an estate agent and that was how I met Cecily. It was me who ended up showing her round a one-bedroom flat in

Hoxton. It was great for getting to Suffolk but completely overpriced and there were problems with the roof. As it happened, it was my birthday that day and I couldn't wait to get out and go to the pub – I was meeting a bunch of friends – so I told her not to buy it and asked her to come with me instead.' He smiled at the memory. 'All my friends loved her. And they all knew we were made for each other.'

'How long after that did you get engaged?'

'Eighteen months. That was too quick for Pauline and Lawrence but we didn't want to hang around. They wanted me to come into the business and I was OK with that. What I was doing in London and what I'm doing here ... they're not so different. It's all about people.'

'So tell me about the actual day of the wedding. Everything that happened.'

The wine was helping. I don't know if Aiden was feeling more comfortable but I certainly was.

'I'll never forget it.' Aiden shook his head. 'Cecily always started the day by reading her horoscope in the newspaper. Well, on that Saturday it said prepare for ups and downs, which is the last thing you want to read on the day of your wedding and it really upset her. Of course, it turned out to be spot-on accurate. I shouldn't say this, but Lawrence and Pauline made a bloody stupid mistake keeping the hotel open. If they hadn't, everything would have been under control and at the end of the day Frank Parris wouldn't have been there and the whole thing would never have happened.'

'When did you meet him?'

'That was on Thursday afternoon, when he arrived. He'd booked a standard room and we'd put him in the

Moonflower Wing. It was a perfectly nice room but he wasn't happy. He wanted something more traditional. So I managed to flip things round and put him in room twelve. That was where he was killed.'

'Describe him for me.'

Aiden considered. 'Fifty years old, curly grey hair, quite short. He was jet-lagged when he arrived and that made him a bit surly. But the next day he was friendlier.'

'You saw him twice?'

'I checked him in. And then Cecily and I met him on Friday lunchtime outside the hotel. He was just getting out of a taxi. He said that he was pleased with the new room and when he heard we were getting married, he couldn't have been nicer. He was quite camp. You could tell he was someone who liked to show off. If you'd told me he was going to be dead in just a few hours' time, I wouldn't have believed you. He was someone who was full of life.'

'Did he say what he'd been doing in Westleton?'

Aiden thought for a moment. 'No. I don't think so. He never mentioned Westleton to me, but he did say he was going to an opera in Snape Maltings that evening. It was something by Mozart. I don't know if he'd come specially for that. But people do drive for miles to come to Snape. Quite a few of them stay with us.'

'And you didn't see him again?'

'I might have. But if I did, I didn't notice him. As you can imagine, Susan, I had quite a lot on my plate.'

'There was a party on Friday night.'

'Friday evening. Yeah – that was Lawrence and Pauline. They wanted everyone to feel part of it. They're good people.

The hotel's their family.' He glanced out of the window as if he had heard something. But there was still no sign of Roxana. 'The party began at about eight thirty and went on for about an hour.'

'Was Stefan there?'

'Yes. Everyone was there. Lionel, Derek, Stefan, Lisa ... No. Not Derek. But everyone else.'

'Did you talk to Stefan?'

Aiden frowned. 'Probably. I don't really remember. I don't think I spent very much time with him because he was on his way out anyway.'

'He was leaving?'

'Hasn't anyone told you? He'd been fired. Lisa didn't like him. She was convinced that he was stealing the petty cash – or something like that. Actually, she didn't need a reason to get rid of him. If Lisa doesn't like you, you're out. Everyone knows that. She doesn't like me very much if you want the truth, but that's probably because I'm married to her sister. She can't bear Cecily having something she hasn't got.'

I wondered why Lisa hadn't mentioned that she'd told Stefan to leave. What had she said over dinner? *We should have fired him right at the start.* ' Maybe she was implying that she had, actually, fired him later, but it seemed to me that she had deliberately avoided mentioning it and that was strange. Apart from anything else, it made it more likely that he would have been tempted to steal from the guests, knowing that he no longer had a job. I'd have thought she would want me to know that.

'Did you see Frank Parris again?' I asked.

'No. I was with Cecily until eight thirty. Then we went to the party. Then we went to bed.'

A thought occurred to me. 'Shouldn't you have slept apart? On the night before your wedding?'

'Why would we want to do that? It was a traditional wedding in lots of ways. That was what Cecily wanted. But we didn't do a hen night or a stag night. And we certainly weren't going to sleep in separate rooms.'

I remembered something that Aiden had just told me. 'You said there were ups and downs. What exactly did you mean?'

'Well, the murder was a pretty big fucking down if you want the truth ... '

'What were the others?'

'You really want to know? They didn't matter.'

'Everything matters. You never know what's going to be relevant.'

He sighed. 'Well, they were just little things. The sort of stuff that can happen at any wedding. First of all, the marquee was late. It didn't arrive until after lunch on the Friday and they had to work all afternoon to get it up. One of the bridesmaids got sick and had to cancel. Cecily thought that was bad luck. And then she got upset because she'd lost a pen that she was going to have with her when we got married in the rose garden.'

'A pen?'

'It belonged to her dad. He collects antique fountain pens. He never stopped going on about it on the day. He'd only just bought it from a dealer in Snape – it was brand new, unused. And it was blue.'

'I'm sorry?' I didn't get it.

'It was old but it was also new. It was borrowed and it was blue!'

'Of course.' I felt like an idiot.

'Anyway, she couldn't find it. Later on we thought Stefan might have nicked it, but there were other things too. A whole box of wine glasses got broken. The cake was wrong. Why am I even telling you this? It was a wedding just like any other.'

'Except someone got killed.'

'Yes.' That sobered him. 'It should have been the happiest day of my life,' he said. 'We got married at midday, in the garden. It wasn't a religious service; neither of us believes in God. Drinks started at about a quarter to one. And then just as we were sitting down for lunch, one of the hotel maids – a woman called Natasha Mälk – came out screaming that someone was dead and that was the end of it. That was the end of my wedding.' He emptied his glass, then pushed it away as if to indicate that he wasn't having any more. 'I loved Cecily more than you can begin to imagine. I still love her. She's smart and beautiful and she's considerate and she puts up with me. We have a wonderful daughter. And now this has happened and it's like my whole life has turned into a fucking nightmare.'

Just then, a car pulled up in the drive, a silver VW Golf Estate. I saw the nanny driving. Roxana was strapped into the back. The car stopped. The nanny got out and Bear, the golden retriever, jumped out too. This, of course, was the dog that had barked in the night. He must have been quite a puppy then. Now he was old, overweight and slow, bear-like in a meandering way.

'Do you mind if we pick this up another time?' Aiden asked.

'Of course.'

'How long are you planning to stay?'

It was a good question. I didn't really know. 'Perhaps an-other week,' I said.

'Thank you. Thank you for trying to help.'

So far I had done nothing.

I left Aiden MacNeil in the kitchen and showed myself out. As I opened the front door, Roxana ran past me, eager to see her father, not even noticing I was there. She was a very pretty girl with a dark complexion and deep brown eyes. He swept her into his arms.

'How's my girl?'

'Daddy!'

'Where have you been?'

'We went to the park. Has Mummy come home?'

'Not yet, baby. They're still looking . . . '

Once outside, I found myself face to face with the nanny, Eloise, who was carrying a blanket and a picnic hamper. For a moment we stood there, unsure which one of us should get out of the other's way.

She was furious. In a way it was a repeat of what had happened that morning with Joanne Williams – yet this was different. The emotion coming from her was so strong, so pronounced, that I was actually quite shocked. And it was coming out of nowhere. The two of us hadn't even met. I have described Eloise as dark and slim, but she was also wraith-like, vengeful, like something out a Greek tragedy. Even on this bright summer's day, she was dressed in shades of grey. She had jet black hair with a silver-grey streak down one side; less Mary Poppins, more Cruella de Vil.

'Who are you?' she asked.

'I'm a friend of the family. I've been asked to help.'

'We don't need help. We just need to be left alone.' She had a French accent that belonged in an art-house film. Her eyes locked on to mine.

I brushed past her and walked back towards the hotel. When I was some distance away, I turned back to take a last look at the house. She was still there, standing on the door-step, watching me, warning me not to come back.

Contacts

From: Craig Andrews <CAndrews13@aol.com>
Sent: 20 June 2016 at 14:03
To: Susan Ryeland <S.Ryeland@polydorus.co.gr>
Subject: RE: Stefan Codrescu

Hi Susan

Surprised to get your email. I see you're using a new email
address. Is that in Greece? I was really sorry to hear what
happened. Actually, what did happen? Everyone has got
different stories. All I know is that I'm sad I don't see you any
more. I used to enjoy our long sessions with Pringles and
Prosecco!

Did you see my new book in the *ST* top ten? Well, for one week
only, but they can still put it on the cover. It's called *Marking
Time*. (Yes – I know. Always 'Time' in the title, and it's the same
character, Christopher Shaw ... Hodder like to keep me in my
comfort zone.)

Stefan Codrescu is being held at HMP Wayland, which is
in Norfolk. If you want to meet him, you'll need to get his
permission or perhaps you can talk to his brief. I checked him
out on the Internet. Are you interested in the murder? I'd love
to know what you're up to. Do give me a shout.

Look after yourself.

Craig

PS If you're in town and you need somewhere to stay, let me
know. I'm on my own at the moment and there's plenty of
room. X

*

Stefan Codrescu
HMP Wayland
Thompson Road
Griston
Thetford IP25 6RL
20 June 2016

Dear Stefan,

You and I have never met but my name is Susan Ryeland
and I used to work in publishing. I was recently approached
by Lawrence and Pauline Treherne who are the owners of
Branlow Hall, where I understand you once worked. As you
may have seen in the newspapers, their daughter, Cecily, has

disappeared and they are very concerned. They think I may be able to help.

The reason they came to me is that my most famous writer was a man called Alan Conway and he wrote a book about Branlow Hall and what happened there eight years ago. Alan is now dead and I can't talk to him, but it seems there may be something in his book that is connected to Cecily Treherne. It may also be relevant to you and to your conviction.

I would very much like to meet you as soon as possible. As I understand it, I can only come to HMP Wayland if you put me on your visiting list. Would you be able to do that? If you want to reach me, you can call me on 07710 514444 or write to me at Branlow Hall.

I look forward to hearing from you.

Best wishes,

Susan Ryeland

*

From: Susan Ryeland <S.Ryeland@polydorus.co.gr>
Sent: 20 June 2016 at 14:18
To: James Taylor <JamesTaylor666!@gmail.com>
Subject: Alan Conway

Dear James

It's been a long time since we saw each other and I hope you haven't changed your email address. How are you? The last time we met was a very drunken dinner at the Crown in Framlingham and you told me you were going back to drama school. Did that ever happen? Should I have seen your name in lights by now?

You're probably wondering why I'm contacting you. It's a long story but somehow I've found myself involved with Alan Conway once again.

He wrote a book called *Atticus Pünd Takes the Case* – this was before the two of you became partners and, of course, before you turned up as Pünd's assistant! It seems that he may have based the book on a real-life story that took place in Suffolk, at a hotel called Branlow Hall. Did he ever mention that name to you? A man called Stefan Codrescu was arrested for murder but it's just possible that he wasn't the real culprit.

I know that Alan kept a lot of notes. I remember going through his study with you when I was looking for information about *Magpie Murders*. I'm assuming that you inherited all his notebooks and things when you took over Abbey Grange and although you may have put the whole lot in a skip, if you have kept anything, it might be helpful.

You can contact me on this email address or on my phone: 07710 514444. It would be good to see you anyway. I'm assuming you're in London. Right now I'm in Suffolk, but I can drop down any time.

Love,
Susan (Ryeland)

*

Fri 20 June, 14:30
Hi Lionel. I'm sending this
from Branlow Hall. Are
you still on this number?
Are you in the UK? Can we meet?
It's about Cecily Treherne.
Very important. Thanks.
Susan Ryeland.

*

From: Susan Ryeland <S.Ryeland@polydorus.co.gr>
Sent: 20 June 2016 at 14:38
To: Kate Leith <Kate@GordonLeith.com>
Subject: Alan Conway

Hi Katie

I'm back in the UK – briefly – and in Suffolk! Sorry I didn't have
time to call or email. It was all very sudden. I'm afraid it's Alan
Conway again. He won't leave me alone.

How are you? And Gordon, Jack, Daisy? It's been ages. You
never did come to Crete!

How about dinner tonight or tomorrow (Saturday)? I can come
over or you can come to me. I'm staying at Branlow Hall (free).
Call or email.

Love
Susan xxx

*

Fri 20 June, 14:32
Hi Susan. Yes. I saw about
Cecily in the papers. Terrible.
Anything I can do to help.
I'm in London. Virgin Active
Barbican. Call or email:
LCorby@virginactive.co.uk any
time. All best. Lionel.

*

From: Susan Ryeland <S.Ryeland@polydorus.co.gr>
Sent: 20 June 2016 at 14:45
To: Lawrence Treherne <lawrence.treherne@Branlow.com>
Subject: Cecily

Dear Lawrence

I hope you're OK and that Pauline is feeling better.

I met Aiden this morning and we had a good chat. I've also managed
to track down Lionel Corby with the number you gave me. He's in
London and I will probably go and see him tomorrow. We could talk
over the phone but I think it's better to see him face to face.

While I'm away, I wonder if I could ask you a favour? Could
you write everything that happened, from your perspective,
on Thursday 14th, Friday 15th and Saturday 16th June? I.e. the

wedding weekend. Did you talk to Frank Parris? Did you see or hear anything the night he was killed? I know this may be a lot to ask but the more people I talk to, the more complicated it all gets and it would be really helpful to have an overview.

Also, I hate to mention this, but I'd be very grateful if you could send me part or all of the payment we agreed. My partner, Andreas, is on his own in Crete and he may need to hire extra people to cover for me. I can give you his bank details if you want to send it electronically.

Thanks.
Susan

PS You said you'd let me have the name of the headmaster who moved out of room 12 when Alan Conway moved in. Did you manage to find it?

*

From: Kate Leith <Kate@GordonLeith.com>
Sent: 20 June 2016 at 15:03
To: Susan Ryeland <S.Ryeland@polydorus.co.gr>
Subject: RE: Alan Conway

Sue!

Can't believe your back and you didn't tell me. Yes. Come tonight – 7 or whenever. What are you doing at Branlow Hall? Glad you're not paying – it's an arm and a leg.

Godron not here, I'm afraid. Working late as usual. Daisy also on her travels but Jack may grace us with an appearance.

Let me know if there's a problem. Otherwise I'll expect youy around 7.

Can't wait to see you.

Katie xxxxx

*

From: Susan Ryeland <S.Ryeland@polydorus.co.gr>
Sent: 20 June 2016 at 15:20
To: Andreas Patakis <Andakis@polydorus.co.gr>
Subject: Missing you

My dearest Andreas

It feels funny to be emailing you. We never send each other emails ... certainly not in the last two years (except that time when you disappeared in Athens and I was about to summon Interpol). But I'm sending out a whole raft of emails and this seems the easiest way.

First of all, I'm missing you. I really am. When I wake up in the morning, the first thing I notice is the empty bed. They've given me an absurd mountain of pillows but it's not the same. I've only been here a couple of days but it feels a long time already. I drove past Cloverleaf when I was in London (it's still in

111

scaffolding) and I had this weird sense that I don't really belong here. I'm not sure where I am any more.

There's not much to tell you about Cecily Treherne. I met her husband, Aiden MacNeil, this morning and I liked him more than I thought I would. I'd certainly be surprised if he had anything to do with her disappearance. I wouldn't say he was in mourning exactly – but he looked quite exhausted. He's got a 7-year-old daughter and a nanny straight out of *The Omen*. And a dog who ought to be a witness as he was actually there, in his basket, on the night Frank Parris died. If only he could talk!

As far as I can see, the police have more or less given up looking for Cecily. DCS Locke is in charge of the case. He was also the detective who investigated Alan's murder and he was pretty useless then. So far we haven't spoken which is probably just as well as – you'll probably remember – we didn't get on.

As to what happened all those years ago, it feels as complicated as an Alan Conway novel but without the usual hints and tips from the author to help me solve it. And if it's true that Stefan Codrescu didn't do it, then once again it's missing the last chapter! I've found out where Stefan is in prison and I've written to him, though I don't know if he'll see me.

But I'm not writing to you about the murder.

It all happened very suddenly, the decision to come back to the UK and I know it's only supposed to be a week, but it has made me think a lot about us and the hotel and Crete. I do love you,

Andreas, and I do want to be with you, but I'm beginning to worry that things aren't working between us ... not the way they used to.

We never have time to talk about anything except business and I sometimes wonder if we're running the hotel or if the hotel is running us. I've tried so hard to keep up my end of things but the two of us are working so hard that we never seem to have time for each other. And I have to be honest. I've spent my entire life in publishing. I've always loved everything about books ... manuscripts, editing, sales conferences, parties. I miss it. I just don't feel fulfilled.

God, that sounds awful. It's all about me! But it isn't. Really it's about us.

I just think we need to sit down and talk about what we're doing, why we're doing it and whether we actually want to go on doing it together. I even wonder how happy you really are at the Polydorus, especially when everything is going wrong. If we've made a mistake, we have to be brave enough to say so. The last thing we want is to end up blaming each other, but sometimes I think that's exactly where we're heading.

Anyway, I'll stop there. I'm off for dinner with Katie. Please don't be cross with me. I just wish things were as they used to be. I wish *Magpie Murders* had never happened. Bloody Alan Conway. It's all his fault.

All my love,
Susan

*

From: Susan Ryeland <S.Ryeland@polydorus.co.gr>
Sent: 20 June 2016 at 15:35
To: Michael Bealey <mbealeyt@orionbooks.com>
Subject: London/help

Michael

I know it's been a while but I'm back in London for a few
days and just wondering if there was anything doing at OB or
Hachette? You may remember you did approach me a couple
of years back. We had that nice lunch at the Wolseley and I was
very tempted ... that was before everything went awry!

Or maybe you've heard if there's anything around? Senior
editor? Commissioning editor? Whatever.

Hope all's well. Nice to see you making money out of Atticus
Pünd – and with the original covers!

Susan X

Three Chimneys

Katie came bounding out of the house as I drove up in the MG and I guessed she must have been listening out for me. It had been two years since I had last seen her and she looked completely unchanged, happy to see me, relaxed. I got out and we embraced.

'You look wonderful. What an amazing tan. Oh my God, really, you look more Greek than English.'

I had brought her olive oil, honey, dried herbs from the village of Kritsa, up in the hills. She gathered them up and led me into the house and I had to admit that, almost for the first time since I had arrived in England, I actually felt welcome.

She had, of course, prepared a perfect meal, perfectly presented in her perfect kitchen. How did she do it? I'd emailed her at two thirty in the afternoon and this was the day she worked at the local garden centre, but even so she'd managed to conjure up a Moroccan chicken tagine with chickpeas, almonds and couscous served with a chilled rosé. I mean, come to my flat in Crouch End and you wouldn't have found even half of the ingredients. Cumin powder? Coriander leaves?

Most of the jars on my spice rack had that sticky, dusty quality that comes from never being opened and you'd have had to root around in the fridge to find a vegetable that wasn't limp, bruised or withered – or all three.

Come to dinner with me and I'd have ordered takeaway, but although I'd offered to take us out to a pub or a restaurant in Woodbridge, she wouldn't hear of it.

'No. We can't talk properly in a restaurant and anyway, Jack will be home later. He'll want to see you.'

Jack was her twenty-one-year-old son, now in his first year at Bristol University. Daisy, nineteen, was on her gap year, helping refugees in northern France.

It's funny how close the two of us have always been, even though we're worlds apart. That was true even when we were children. We grew up together in a very ordinary house in north London. We went to the same school. We swapped clothes and made jokes about each other's boyfriends. But while Katie was completely happy, dreaming of the day when she would have a home and a lifestyle almost identical to the one our parents had foisted on us, I was escaping to my local library and my dreams were of a very different nature. I would join a gang at Jamaica Inn, preying on the wretched sailors who came too close. I would fall madly in love with Edward Rochester, but in my version of the story I would save him from the flames. I would travel to the lost city of Kôr and find immortality in the Pillar of Fire. We were the complete opposite of Cecily and Lisa Treherne, who had been two sisters at war, actually throwing knives. Katie and I had nothing in common except our fondness for each other and that had lasted throughout our lives.

There were times when I wished I was more like her. Katie's life was a model of comfort and orderliness: the two children now entering their twenties, the accountant husband who spent three nights a week in London but who was still devoted to her after a marriage that had lasted a quarter of a century, the part-time job, the close circle of friends, the community work ... all the rest of it. I often thought of her as a smarter, more grown-up version of myself.

And yet I couldn't have lived in a house like this. I wouldn't even have bought a house that had a name. Numbers were good enough for the likes of me.

Three Chimneys was in a quiet crescent just outside Woodbridge and yes, it did have three chimneys, even if they were completely useless because all the fireplaces had been filled in with those gas-effect fires. Looking at all the polished surfaces, the sliding glass doors, the thick-pile carpets and tasteful art, I knew that if I had lived here I would have felt trapped, but Katie didn't seem to mind. She was a mother, a wife, a housewife. She liked to be defined.

Not that I would hold up my own, chaotic lifestyle as anything to be envied. My early love of books hadn't taken me to the places of my imagination. It had taken me into ... books. I'd started as a junior editor at HarperCollins, then commissioning editor, then editorial director and finally Head of Fiction at a company that had, literally, gone up in flames. The publishing industry is full of idealists, people who love what they do, which is why so many of us are badly paid. I was lucky to buy a two-bedroom flat in Crouch End before prices went insane but I'd never paid off the mortgage, not until the day I sold it. I'd had plenty of relationships but they'd never lasted because I didn't want them to. At least Andreas had changed that.

So there we were. Two sisters looking at each other across a divide that had widened as we had grown older, far apart and yet close. We made judgements about each other, but perhaps those judgements told us more about ourselves.

'Do you think it's sensible, getting yourself involved in another murder enquiry?' Katie asked.

'I'll be more careful this time.'

'I hope so.'

'Anyway, I'm beginning to think the whole thing may be a waste of time.'

She was surprised. 'Why do you say that?'

'Because the more questions I ask, the more likely it seems to me that it was Stefan Codrescu who killed Frank Parris. All the evidence is stacked up against him, and as far as I can see there were only two people who had any motive, and I'm not even sure what that motive was.'

'Who are they?'

'Oh ... a couple who live in Westleton. Joanne and Martin. She was Frank's sister.'

Katie looked surprised. 'Joanne and Martin Williams?'

'Do you know them?'

'I met them once. I can't say I really liked them.' That was unusual. Katie always thought the best of everyone.

'Why was that?' I asked.

'It was nothing personal. They just weren't my type.' She saw that I wanted more and continued, reluctantly. 'She was a real ball-breaker. She dominated the table ... never let anyone get a word in edgeways. And he was a complete doormat. She walked all over him. She seemed to revel in it.'

That puzzled me. 'When did you last see them?' I asked.

'Oh ... it was ages ago. Maybe even before the murder. They were at a dinner and I only remember them because I joked about it afterwards. I didn't understand how two people like that could possibly stay married to each other!'

'And she was the one in control?'

'Absolutely.'

'It's strange because I saw them this morning and if any-thing, I'd say it was the other way round.' I put them out of my mind. 'It has to be Stefan,' I said. 'I mean ... blood on the pillow, blood in the shower, money under the mattress. He was even seen going into the room!'

'In that case, what happened to Cecily Treherne?'

'It could just be a coincidence. She could have fallen into the river. She could have gone for a swim and drowned. According to her sister, the marriage wasn't everything it was cracked up to be and she could have run off with some-body else.' Even as I said that, I knew it was impossible. She wouldn't have left her daughter behind.

'Will they still pay you if you don't get a result?'

That was something I hadn't considered. I reached for my cigarettes. 'Do you mind if I step outside? I want one of these.'

Katie gave me a sideways look. 'You said you were think-ing of giving up.'

'I did think about it.'

'So what happened?'

'I decided not to.'

She passed me an ashtray. She'd known I was going to use it. Then she put a percolator of coffee, milk and two mugs on a tray and – unusually for her – two tumblers of whisky. 'Will you join me?' she asked.

'Just a small one. I'm driving.'

We went outside and sat at a wooden table beside the fish pond. It was a warm evening with a half-moon and a few stars. The garden looked beautiful, of course, filled with plants that Katie got at half price from her work. She had recently bought a statue of a leaping frog with water gushing out of its mouth and the sound of it only made the silence around us more profound. I noticed that one bush had died. It was very prominent, in a circular bed in the middle of the lawn. I wouldn't have been able to put a name to it – it was round and tightly cropped – but it was completely brown. For some reason, it troubled me. I would have thought Katie would have got rid of it the moment the first leaves began to droop.

I lit a cigarette and smoked peacefully, listening to the falling water.

'You are going back to Crete?' she asked.

Katie and I had no secrets from each other. We had talked about the hotel, the problems, my misgivings, while we ate.

'I don't know,' I said. 'I don't even know where I am with Andreas. Before we left England, he asked me to marry him.'

'You told me. You turned him down.'

'I said yes. But later on we both changed our minds. We didn't think marriage would suit us. I made him take the ring back. It was much more than he could afford anyway and we need every penny we can get.' I examined her over the tip of my cigarette. 'Sometimes I wish I could be more like you.'

'You know that's not true.' She looked away.

'No. I mean it. There are times when I just feel completely worn out. I don't know if I want to be with Andreas any more. I don't know what I want.'

'Listen to me, Susan. Forget this stupid murder investigation.' She had turned back and her eyes locked on to mine. 'Go back to Greece. You don't belong in England any more. Go back to Andreas.'

'Why do you say that?'

'Because he's a good man and you don't want to lose him. Honestly, I was so glad when you met him. I was the one who introduced you!'

'That's not true. It was Melissa ... '

'Well, you'd never have met him if I hadn't sent Jack and Daisy to Woodbridge School. Trust me. When you've got someone like Andreas in your life, you should count your blessings. But that's how you've always been. You're always thinking ahead, planning for the future. You never actually sit back and enjoy what you have.'

I was puzzled. I thought she was trying to tell me something quite different but she wasn't putting it into words. 'Katie, is everything all right?' I asked.

She sighed. 'Do you ever think about your age?' she asked.

'I try not to. Don't forget I'm two years older than you.'

'I know. But there are times when I can't stop myself.' She tried to make light of it. 'I hate the idea of getting old. I'm getting to the age when I look around me at this house, this garden and I think to myself ... is this it?'

'But it's everything you ever wanted, isn't it?'

'Yes. I suppose so. I've been lucky.'

A silence fell between us. For some reason it wasn't a very comfortable one.

'Did you tell Sajid Khan where to find me?' I'm not sure why I blurted the question out just then but it had been in the back of my mind ever since Lawrence and Pauline Treherne had turned up at the hotel. How had they found me? They had said that Khan had given them my address, but he didn't have it. Only Katie did.

'Sajid Khan? The solicitor?' I could see I had thrown her. 'He helped us when we had that unfair-dismissal thing at the garden centre and I see him now and then. But I don't think I said anything. Was he the one who got you into all this?'

'Apparently.'

'Well, I hope you're not blaming me. Maybe it was Gordon. He can't keep anything secret.'

Our conversation was interrupted by the sound of a motorbike pulling up. 'That's Jack,' Katie said. She sounded relieved.

A few moments later, Jack came through the garden gate, wearing a leather jacket and carrying a helmet. It was two years since I had seen him and I was a little thrown by his appearance. His hair was long and quite skanky. He hadn't shaved and the stubble didn't suit him. He came over and kissed me on both cheeks and I smelled alcohol and cigarette smoke on his breath. I was hardly in any position to judge him, but I was still surprised. He had never smoked in his teens. Looking at him, I thought a light had been switched off in his eyes. He seemed almost nervous, as if he hadn't expected to find me there.

'Hi, Susan,' he said.

'Hi, Jack. How are you?'

'I'm good. How's Crete?'

'It's OK.'

'Mum. Is there anything in the fridge?'

'There's some chicken. And you can finish the pasta if you like.'

'Thanks.' He half smiled at me. 'It's great to see you, Susan.'

And then he was gone, shuffling off towards the kitchen. I watched him leave, remembering the ten-year-old discovering *The Lord of the Rings*, the twelve-year-old shouting and laughing in the back of my new MG, the fifteen-year-old sweating over his GCSEs. Was this just part of the natural process of growing up or was I missing something?

Katie must have seen what I was thinking. 'It's all been a bit much for him, his first year at uni,' she said. 'When he comes home, all he wants is food, laundry and bed. But he'll be all right in a couple of weeks. He just needs a bit of TLC.'

'I'm surprised you let him buy a motorbike.' It was none of my business but I knew how much Katie must have hated the idea. She'd always worried — almost obsessively — about either of her children getting hurt.

She made a helpless gesture. 'He's twenty-one. He saved up for it himself. How was I going to stop him?' She put down her drink, somehow signalling that the evening was over. 'I'm sorry, Susan. I ought to go in and look after him.'

'That's OK. I'm going to London tomorrow. I've got an early start. Thanks for dinner.'

'It's been lovely to see you – but please think about what I said. Honestly, I don't think you're going to find Cecily Treherne. Maybe nobody will. And Frank Parris was killed a long time ago. You're better off out of it.'

We kissed and went our separate ways.

It was only as I drove away that I realised that the whole evening had been out of kilter, almost from the start. Katie had been trying too hard. It was as if the chicken tagine, the pink wine, the paper napkins and all the rest of it had been set out deliberately to distract me, that they were somehow fake ... like the three chimneys on the roof.

I thought about the dead bush – the broom or the briar or whatever it was – sitting there untended in the middle of the lawn. And then I remembered the email she had sent me with no fewer than three typos. *Godron not here, I'm afraid*. Well, anyone can make mistakes. She had probably been in a hurry. But that wasn't Katie. She was always so precise.

Maybe I'd spent too much time playing detective, talking to people who seemed polite and pleasant on the face of it but who might turn out to be cold-blooded killers. But I couldn't help myself. I was sure Katie was hiding something. She wasn't telling me the truth.

Nightcaps

It was late when I got back to the hotel and I'd intended to go straight to bed, but coming in through the entrance hall, I noticed Aiden MacNeil, sitting on his own in the bar, and it was too good an opportunity to miss. I went in.

'Do you mind if I join you?'

I'd already sat down before he could answer but in fact he was pleased to see me. 'I'd be glad of the company,' he said.

The bar had the feel of a gentleman's club but a very empty one: we were the only guests, sitting there surrounded by leather armchairs, occasional tables, rugs and lots of wood panelling. A grandfather clock ticked in the corner, sonorously reminding us that it was twenty past ten. Aiden was wearing a cashmere jumper and jeans, moccasins but no socks. He had been cradling a tumbler of some colourless liquid that certainly wasn't water. I also noticed a paperback book, which he had turned face down. It was the copy of *Atticus Pünd Takes the Case* that he'd shown me earlier.

'What are you drinking?' I asked.

'Vodka.'

Lars was behind the bar. He and Inga seemed to be all over the hotel, like extras from *The Midwich Cuckoos*. 'I'll have a double whisky and another vodka for Mr MacNeil,' I said. I glanced at the book. 'Are you reading it?'

'Rereading it. For about the tenth time. I keep thinking that if Cecily found something in it then maybe I can find it too.'

'And?'

'Nothing. I don't usually read murder mysteries and I still think Alan Conway was a complete bastard, but I have to admit he knew how to tell a story. I like stories set in little communities where no one tells the truth. And it has some great twists – the ending has a real sucker punch . . . at least it did the first time I read it. What I don't understand is why he had to be so fucking spiteful.'

'What do you mean?'

'Listen to this.' He had folded down the corner of one of the pages. He opened it and began to read. '"For all his faults, Algernon was well spoken. He had been educated at a small private school in West Kensington and he could be charming and witty when he wanted to be. With his fair hair cut short and his matinée-idol good looks, he was naturally attractive, particularly to older women who took him at face value and didn't make too many enquiries about his past. He still re-membered buying his first suit on Savile Row. It had cost him much more than he could afford, but, like the car, it made a statement. When he walked into a room, people noticed him. When he talked, they listened."'

He put the book down.

'That's me,' he said. 'Algernon Marsh.'

'Do you think so?'

'He works as an estate agent. So did I. He looks like me. He's even got my initials. I don't know why he's got such a stupid name, though.'

He had a point. During the editing process I had urged Alan to change the name of Algernon, which I'd said sounded like something out of a Noël Coward play. 'Even Agatha Christie didn't have a character called Algernon,' I'd told him, but he hadn't listened, of course.

'Alan had a strange sense of humour,' I said. 'If it makes you feel any better, I turned up in one of his books too.'

'Really?'

'Yes. Sarah Lamb in *Gin & Cyanide*. Ryeland is a breed of sheep, apparently. She's a complete monster and she gets murdered near the end.' The drinks arrived. Aiden finished the one in front of him and went on to the next. 'Did you spend much time with Alan when he came here?'

'No.' Aiden shook his head. 'I met him twice: once when I helped sort out his new room and then again for about five minutes. I didn't terribly like him. He said he was a friend of Frank Parris and that he just wanted to know what had happened, but he was asking all these questions and right from the start I got the feeling he had another agenda. He spent more time with Lawrence and Pauline. And with Cecily. They were stupid to trust him because he went away and wrote a book about us.' He paused. 'How well did you know him?'

'I was his editor – but we were never close.'

'Are all writers like that? Stealing things from the world around them?'

'Every writer is different,' I said. 'But they don't steal, exactly. They absorb. It's such a strange profession, really, living in a sort of twilight between the world they belong to and the world they create. On the one hand, they're monstrous egotists. Self-confidence, self-examination, self-hatred even ... but it's all about *self*. All those hours on their own! And yet at the same time, they're genuinely altruistic. All they want to do is please other people. I've often thought it must demand a sort of deficiency to be a writer. There's something missing in your life so you fill it with words. God knows, I couldn't do it, as much as I love reading. That's why I became an editor. I get all the rewards and the excitement of creating a new book but my job's more fun.'

I sipped my drink. Lars had given me a single malt from the Isle of Jura. I could taste the peat.

'Mind you, Alan Conway was like no writer I ever met,' I continued. 'He didn't like writing – or at least, he didn't like the books that had made him successful. He thought detective fiction was beneath him. That's one of the reasons he put you and this hotel into his novel. I think he enjoyed playing with you, turning you into Algernon, because to him the whole thing was just a game.'

'What were the other reasons?'

'I'll tell you, although I've never told anyone else. He was already running out of ideas. It was as simple as that. He actually stole the plot of his fourth book, *Night Comes Calling*, from someone he taught on a writers' course. I met them and I read their original manuscript. I think he came to Branlow Hall partly out of curiosity – he knew Frank Parris – but mainly because he was looking for inspiration for his next book.'

'But somehow he found out who the real killer was. At least, that was what Cecily believed. Isn't that what this is all about?'

I shook my head. 'I don't know, Aiden. He could have found something. But it's equally possible that he wrote it without even knowing what he was doing. When Cecily read the book, a word or a description could have stirred up a memory or triggered an association that only she knew about. I mean, if Alan had worked out that Stefan Codrescu hadn't killed Frank Parris, wouldn't he have told someone? It wouldn't have harmed his sales. It might even have helped them. What possible reason could he have had for keeping silent?'

'But in that case, what did Cecily read? And what's happened to her?'

I had no answer to that.

Behind the bar, Lars had been wiping a glass. He set it down and called out to us. 'Last orders in five minutes, Mr MacNeil.'

'That's OK, Lars. I think we're finished. You can start to close down now.'

'I haven't asked you about Cecily,' I said. This was the conversation I was most nervous about but we seemed to be comfortable with each other and this had to be the right time. 'What happened on that last day ... '

'Wednesday.' He spoke the single word in a low voice, gazing into his drink, and I felt a distinct change in the atmosphere between us as I moved into painful territory.

'Do you mind talking about it?'

He hesitated. 'I've already gone over it, again and again, with the police. I don't see how it will help. It's got nothing to do with you.'

'That's true. And I know it's none of my business. But I'm worried about her too and if there's anything you can remember, any small detail, even if you think it's irrelevant, you never know ... '

'All right.' He called over to Lars. 'Lars – I'll have one more before you close.' He glanced at me. 'You?'

'No. I'm OK, thanks.'

He steeled himself. 'I don't really know what to tell you, Susan. It was a very ordinary day. I mean, that's the hell of it. It was just another Wednesday and I had absolutely no idea that my whole fucking life was about to be torn apart. That afternoon, Eloise took Roxie to the GP. It wasn't anything very important – just a tummy upset.'

'Tell me about Eloise.'

'What do you want to know?'

'How long has she been with you?'

'From the very start. She arrived after Roxie was born.'

'Roxana's a pretty name.'

'Yes. Cecily chose it.'

'So Eloise came to Suffolk the year after Frank Parris was killed?'

'That's right. Roxana was born in January 2009. She arrived a couple of months after that.'

'Was she in England at the time of the murder?'

'You don't think she had anything to do with it, do you? I'm sorry, but that's crazy. Eloise Radmani is from Marseille. She never knew Frank Parris. And actually how she got here is a very sad story. She was married. She met her husband in London – they were both students. But he died.'

'What of?'

'AIDS. He'd had a stomach ulcer and needed a blood transfusion. He was very unlucky. He died in France, but after that she decided to come back to England and joined a nanny agency.'

'Which agency?'

'Knightsbridge Knannies.' He spelled out the second word so that I would get the joke.

I didn't smile. I was still remembering the way Eloise had looked at me as I left the house – utterly vengeful. 'So on the day Cecily disappeared, she took Roxana to the doctor.'

'After lunch. Yes. I'd taken the dog out in the morning ... just round the grounds. It was Cecily's turn in the afternoon. She was in and out of the hotel during the day. We both were. It's not too far to go.'

'Did she talk about the book with you?'

'No.'

'Did you know that she'd sent a copy to her parents in the South of France?'

Aiden shook his head. 'The police asked me that,' he said. 'Pauline told them about the telephone call. Of course she did. I mean, was it really a coincidence that on the Tuesday she rings her parents to tell them about this stupid novel and the very next day—' He broke off and drank some of the vodka, the ice rattling against the side of the glass. 'For what it's worth, Detective Chief Superintendent Locke doesn't think there's any connection. His theory is that if Cecily was attacked, it was by someone completely random.'

'What do you think?'

'I don't know. But the answer to your question is – no, she didn't say anything about posting the book. Maybe she thought I wouldn't take her seriously. Or maybe it was because she knew I'd never had any time for Stefan Codrescu, so she didn't think I'd be interested.' He reached out and closed the book. 'It hurts me that she didn't confide in me. It makes me feel responsible.'

'When was the last time you saw her?' I asked.

'I don't know why you're asking me these questions. I don't understand what you want to know!' He stopped himself. 'I'm sorry. It's just very difficult.' He finished his drink just as Lars brought over the last one he had ordered. He took it gratefully, pouring the contents into the glass he had just emptied. 'The last time I saw her was about three o'clock in the afternoon,' he said. 'She took the VW. I went out about half an hour later in the Range Rover. I had to go over to Framlingham. I had a meeting with our solicitor, a man called Sajid Khan.'

It was funny the way Sajid Khan's name kept cropping up. He was Alan Conway's old solicitor. He had told the Trehernes where to find me. He was working for Martin and Joanne Williams. My sister, Katie, had used him. And now, on the day of Cecily's disappearance, Aiden was telling me he'd been to see him too.

'There were some papers to sign,' he went on. 'Nothing very important. And I had a few errands to run. Cecily had asked me to drop some clothes into the charity shop. She's a big supporter of EACH.'

'Each?'

'East Anglia's Children's Hospices. There isn't a branch in Woodbridge. I had to pick up a chair which we'd had re-upholstered. I went to the supermarket too. I got home at fiveish. Maybe half past. I was surprised Cecily wasn't there. Inga was making Roxie her tea. She comes in and helps sometimes.'

'Where was Eloise?'

'She had the evening off.' He lifted his glass and emptied it. I did the same. 'When Cecily still hadn't got home at seven o'clock, I went looking for her in the hotel. Sometimes she'd work in the main office and lose track of the time. But she wasn't there. Nobody had seen her. I still wasn't too worried. I mean, this is Suffolk. Nothing much happens in Suffolk.'

Both Frank Parris and Alan Conway had been murdered in Suffolk, but I decided not to mention it.

'I rang a few of her friends. I tried calling Lisa but I couldn't get hold of her. I was thinking something might have happened to Bear. He's getting on a bit and sometimes he has trouble with his hips. Anyway, at eight o'clock, when I still hadn't heard from her, I made a decision and called the police.'

He fell silent. That had been when the long silence had begun.

I was trying to work out the timings. He'd left the hotel at approximately half past three. He was back sometime after five; maybe as late as five thirty. Framlingham was about twenty minutes from Woodbridge. That felt about right for a couple of errands and a meeting.

'What time did you meet Sajid Khan?' I asked.

He gave me a peculiar look and I knew I'd asked one question too many. 'Why do you want to know?'

'I'm just trying to—'

But he didn't let me finish. 'You think I killed her, don't you?'

'No.' I denied it but I didn't sound convincing.

'Yes, you do. When did I leave? When was the last time I saw her? You think the police haven't asked me the same questions over and over again? Everyone thinks I killed her, the one woman who actually made me happy, and that's what they're going to think for the rest of my life. My daughter is going to grow up wondering if her daddy killed her mummy and I'm never going to be able to explain ... '

He got unsteadily to his feet and I was shocked to see tears streaming down his cheeks.

'You have no right,' he continued hoarsely. 'You have no right at all. I don't mind getting it from the police. That's their job. But who are you? You're the one who caused all the trouble in the first place. You were the one who published the book – turning what happened here into some sort of entertainment. And now you come here like Sherlock Holmes or Atticus fucking Pünd asking me questions that have got nothing to do with you. If you can find something in the book, then get on with it. Do what you've been paid to do. But from now on, leave me alone!'

He left. I watched him weave his way out of the room. Behind me, Lars brought a metal shutter rattling down and crashing against the bar. Suddenly I was on my own.

Framlingham

I felt sorry for Aiden and worried that I'd gone too far. But that didn't stop me checking out his story the next day.

It was strange being back in Framlingham, the market town that Alan Conway had chosen as his home and where I had spent so much time immediately following his death. I parked on the main square opposite the Crown, where I had stayed and where I had enjoyed a remarkably drunken meal with James Taylor, Alan's partner. It reminded me that I still hadn't heard back from him and I wondered if he had received my email. I wanted to stretch my legs so I walked up the High Street, past the cemetery where Alan was buried. I thought about visiting his grave – I could see it between two yew trees – but decided against it. We'd always had a difficult, edgy relationship and if I'd gone to have a quiet chat at the gravestone there was every chance it would have turned into a quarrel.

Framlingham seemed quieter than ever. Despite its wonderful castle and surrounding countryside, it suffers from a strange midweek emptiness. It's hard to tell if the shops are open and frankly, it's hard to care. There's a country market every weekend but otherwise the main square is little more than a car park. The supermarket that Aiden had visited is right in the middle but hides away as if it knows how ugly it is and feels ashamed to be there.

The EACH charity shop was at the bottom end of the town, just along the road from an estate agent. It was quite small, occupying what must once have been a cottage, one of four identical buildings in a little terrace, but someone had imposed four large, modern windows in the front, completely divorcing it from its neighbours. I'm afraid I find charity shops quite dispiriting. There are so many of them and at the end of the day, each one is a reminder of a failed business and the general collapse of the High Street. But this one had a cheerful volunteer called Stavia, lots of books and toys and three racks of surprisingly high-end clothes. There was no one else in there apart from the two of us and Stavia was keen to talk. In fact, once she'd started, it was hard to get her to stop.

'Aiden MacNeil? Yes, of course I remember him. I was here when he came in and afterwards I had to speak to the police. Isn't it awful, what's happened! You don't usually get that sort of thing in Suffolk, although there was that business in Earl Soham all those years ago and the death of that writer. Yes, Mr MacNeil came in that Wednesday afternoon. I saw him park his car on the other side of the road – just over there.

'He brought in four or five dresses, some jerseys, shirts. Some of them were quite old but there was a Burberry dress that had never been worn. It still had the label. We sold it almost at once for a hundred pounds, which is a lot more than we usually get for anything off the rail. The police wanted to know who bought it but I couldn't help them because they'd paid cash. They took her other clothes away – the ones we hadn't sold – and we never saw them again, which I think is a little unfair, although I suppose I can't complain, given the circumstances. Oh – and there were some men's clothes too. A jacket, some ties, an old shirt and a very nice waistcoat.'

'Did you talk to him?'

'Yes. We did have a chat. He was a very nice man, very friendly. He told me he was going to pick up a chair. He'd had it resprung or something. He said that his wife was a big supporter of EACH and had donated quite a bit of money to our Treehouse Appeal. I can't believe he had anything to do with her disappearance. I mean, he couldn't have just stood here and chatted if he had, could he?'

'Do you remember what time he was here?'

'It was four o'clock. I know because I remember thinking that I only had half an hour until we closed and that was when he walked in. Why are you so interested in all this, by the way? Are you a journalist? I hope I'm not going to get into any trouble talking about it all ... '

I managed to reassure her and, partly out of guilt, spent five pounds on a Mexican pot with a cactus that turned out to be fake. I donated it to another charity shop on the way back to the car.

After that, I walked back up to the street with the mustard yellow building that housed Wesley & Khan Solicitors. It was two years since I had been there and I had a strange sense of déjà vu coming off the main road into what must have once been a private house. In fact, I was quite sure that it was the same bored girl sitting behind the reception desk: not only that, she might have been reading the same magazine. It was as if time had stood still. The potted plants were still half-dead. The atmosphere was as vacant as I remembered.

I had actually phoned ahead for an appointment this time and I was shown upstairs the moment I arrived, the uneven floorboards creaking under my feet. It struck me that there were two mysteries attached to the practice of Wesley & Khan. Who was Mr Wesley? Did he even exist? And how had a man like Khan, of proudly Indian ethnicity, managed to end up in a place like Framlingham? Suffolk is not racist. But it is fairly white.

Sajid Khan was exactly how I remembered him, dark and ebullient, with heavy eyebrows that almost met in the middle of his forehead, leaping up from behind his impressively large desk – fake antique – and bounding across the room to take my one proffered hand in both of his.

'My dear Ms Ryeland, what a pleasure to see you again! And staying at Branlow Hall, I understand! How very much like you to get yourself involved once again in Suffolk skulduggery.' He led me to a chair. 'Will you have some tea?'

'I'm fine, thank you.'

'I insist.' He pressed a key on his telephone. 'Tina, could you bring up tea for two?' He beamed at me. 'How is Crete?'

'It's lovely, thank you.'

'I have never been there. We normally go to Portugal for the summer. But if you're running a hotel, maybe we should give you a try.'

He sat down behind the desk. The photograph frame was still there, the one with the digital pictures sliding across the screen. I wondered if he had added new ones in the two years since I had been here. Looking at them, they seemed the same. His wife, his children, his wife and his children, him and his wife ... an endless merry-go-round of memories.

'That was an extraordinary business with Alan Conway,' he continued, more serious now. 'I never actually learned what happened, but I was led to believe that you were almost killed.' He raised an eyebrow and the other one went with it. 'Are you all right now?'

'Yes. I'm fine.'

'I haven't heard from the young man who was his partner for a while. James Taylor. He ended up with all the money, as I'm sure I don't need to remind you. The last I heard, he was in London, spending his way through his inheritance as fast as he could.' He smiled. 'So how can I help you this time round? You mentioned Cecily MacNeil on the telephone.'

It was the first time I had heard her called that. To everyone else she was Cecily Treherne, as if the marriage had never happened.

'Yes,' I said. 'Her parents came to see me in Crete. Strangely enough, Alan may be involved again. You know that he wrote a book partly based on what happened at Branlow Hall?'

'I know. I read it. And I may be completely obtuse but I never actually got the connection. It never occurred to me that he was writing about Branlow Hall. The book wasn't set in Suffolk, of course, and there wasn't any wedding or anything like that. It was somewhere in Devon.'

'Tawleigh-on-the-Water.'

'That's right. Nobody was mentioned in it by name.'

'He always changed the names. I think he was probably afraid of being sued.' It was time to get to the point. I was planning to drive to London and I wanted to be on my way. 'Lawrence and Pauline Treherne think that Cecily noticed something in the book and that it may be connected to her disappearance. Do you mind if I ask you a few questions?'

He spread his hands. 'Please fire away. I'm afraid I didn't help you very much last time. Perhaps this time I can do better.'

'OK. I want to start with Aiden. He came to see you on the day Cecily disappeared.'

'Yes. That's right.'

'Do you remember what time?'

Khan looked surprised at that, as if it wasn't something I should have asked. 'Five o'clock,' he said. 'It was a short meeting. A contract with a new supplier.' He paused. 'I hope you don't think that he had anything to do with his wife's disappearance.'

'Not exactly, no. But the day before she went missing, Cecily rang her parents. She believed she'd found new evidence about the murder of Frank Parris eight years before and she didn't tell Aiden—'

'I think I should stop you there, Ms Ryeland. First of all, Mr MacNeil is a client of this firm, and anyway, he had absolutely no reason whatsoever to murder Frank Parris, if that's what you're suggesting.'

The door opened and the young woman from the reception desk came in with two mugs of tea and a bowl of sugar on a tray. The mugs were white with the logo W&K printed on the side.

'What happened to Mr Wesley?' I asked as he passed one of them over.

'He retired.' Khan smiled at the girl. 'Thank you, Tina.'

I waited until she had gone, then continued more carefully. 'Were you here in Framlingham at the time of the murder?' I asked.

'Yes. I was. As a matter of fact, I spoke to Mr Parris. We had a brief conversation the day before he died.'

'Really?' That came as a surprise.

'Yes. I was asked to contact him on a personal matter. It was to do with an inheritance. I don't need to go into the details.'

'You were acting for Martin and Joanne Williams,' I said. I was bluffing, really. I remembered seeing his business card in their kitchen and knew he had to be referring to them. 'I went to Heath House,' I added. 'They explained it all to me.'

'How are they?'

'Very well. In fact, your ears should have been burning. They were very appreciative about what you did for them.' Now I was outright lying. Martin and Joanne hadn't told me anything very much. I just hoped that if I flattered Khan enough, I might draw some of the information out of him.

It worked. 'Well, in the end I didn't do very much for them,' he said, but in a way that suggested how pleased he was with himself. 'They told you about the house?'

'Yes.'

'The will was absolutely clear. Heath House was given fifty-fifty to the two children: Frank Parris and his sister. Just because Mr Parris had allowed them to live there, rent-free, since his mother's death, I'm afraid that did not constitute an agreement, oral or otherwise. At no point had Mr Parris relinquished his rights.'

I was trying to keep a poker face but in fact Khan had just provided me with a piece of information that might change everything. *'He had this idea of starting another agency and he wanted us to invest.'* That was what Martin had said, but he had been deliberately vague, borderline dishonest. Frank Parris had gone bust and he wanted his share of the house. That was the reason he had come to Suffolk. It might also be the reason why he was killed.

'They do love that house,' I said.

'Oh yes. Joanne grew up in it. It's a lovely place.'

Mrs Khan slid across the photograph frame, dressed in a swimming costume and holding a plastic spade.

'So you spoke to Frank Parris,' I went on.

'I called him on his mobile. This was on the Friday, just after he had visited his sister. He was planning to put the house on the market with Clarke's in Framlingham. I have to say that he was quite abrasive, but then I understand things hadn't gone well for him in Australia. I asked him to give Mr and Mrs Williams a little more time to come to terms with the move and, for that matter, to find somewhere else to live. In this, I was partially successful. He still wanted to contact Clarke's, but he agreed on a long exchange.'

'They must have been very upset.'

'Mrs Williams was not at all pleased.' He added a heaped spoonful of sugar to his tea.

I could easily imagine it. *'Piss off and leave us alone.'* I remembered her parting words. 'They can't have been too sorry when he was beaten to death,' I remarked. I'd learned what I needed to know. There was no need to mince my words.

Khan looked suitably pained. 'I'm not sure that's true. They were family and they were close. Mr and Mrs Williams had lived rent-free for ten years. They really had nothing to complain about.'

I hadn't drunk any of my tea but I didn't want it. I was wondering if Martin or Joanne had popped into Branlow Hall at the time of the murder and how I could find out. Frank Parris might have told them which room he was staying in, but if either of them had decided to kill him, they would have needed to know how to find it. I tried to imagine one or even both of them creeping round the hotel with a hammer, accidentally stepping on Bear's tail as they made their way along the corridor. Somehow, it felt unlikely. But there was nobody else with such an obvious motive.

'Thank you very much, Mr Khan,' I said. I got to my feet, ending the meeting.

He stood up too and we shook hands. 'How is your sister?' he asked.

'I saw her yesterday. She's very well, thank you.'

'I hope things have worked out with Wilcox,' he continued and then, seeing the look of surprise on my face: 'But perhaps the two of you didn't discuss it.'

'Discuss what?' I asked.

He smiled, trying to pretend that it was nothing very serious, but he had made a mistake and he knew it. He did his best to back-pedal. 'Oh, I just gave her some advice,' he said.

'Is she a client?'

The smile was still there, but faltering. 'You'd have to ask her that, Ms Ryeland. I'm sure you understand.'

If she wasn't his client, he could simply have said so.

I had known that something was wrong after the evening I'd spent with Katie. Was Jack in some sort of trouble? Did she have money problems? What was it that she hadn't told me? As I walked back to the car, Martin and Joanne Williams, Frank Parris, Branlow Court and even Cecily Treherne suddenly seemed less important.

My sister was in trouble. I needed to know why.

Martlesham Heath

I was on my way to London.

More emails had come in ... though nothing from Andreas. That didn't surprise me. He never responded very quickly at the best of times and he had a strange reticence when it came to matters that were personal or emotional. He needed time to think about things.

But James Taylor was thrilled I was back in the UK. We would be delighted to see me again and he would bring along anything he could find relating to *Atticus Pünd Takes the Case*. He suggested dinner at Le Caprice and I just hoped that he would be the one who picked up the bill. I had a meeting arranged with Lionel Corby at the gym where he now worked. And Michael Bealey had invited me for 'a quick drink' at Soho House in Greek Street.

Finally, I had called Craig Andrews. There was a possibility I might be in London for quite a few days and I wasn't too tempted by the comforts of the Premier Inn. In his original email, he had offered me a room and I remembered visiting him once in a handsome Victorian house off

Ladbroke Grove. The money hadn't come from his books, incidentally, but from his former career in banking. The Christopher Shaw novels were solid, mid-list titles, nothing more, but they had given him the freedom to enjoy the money he had already made. Craig was more than pleased to put me up and it was good talking to him again on the phone, but why did I feel a pang of guilt as I hung up? It was ridiculous. All I was expecting was a spare room for a couple of nights and maybe supper and a shared bottle of wine.

I stopped off at Woodbridge before I hit the A12. I'd been just about presentable when I was at the hotel, and Katie, of course, hadn't cared what I looked like, but there was no way I was walking into Le Caprice – or, for that matter, Craig's house – in the clothes I'd brought with me. There were a couple of surprisingly good boutiques in the old square and I came away with a knee-length cocktail dress in midnight-blue velvet and a Ralph Lauren cotton jacket (25 per cent off). I'd spent much more than I'd intended, but I reminded myself of the money Lawrence owed me and just hoped it would arrive before my next credit card bill.

With the bags safely stowed away in the boot I was once again on my way south, but just a few miles outside Woodbridge I came to a roundabout and a sign for Martlesham Heath. On an impulse I hit the indicator and took the third exit. Like it or not – and the truth was, I didn't much – there was one encounter that had to take place. I couldn't put it off any longer.

The Suffolk Constabulary headquarters were based in a really ugly modern building about five minutes from the main road. It was a square block of concrete and plate glass that managed to avoid any architectural merit whatsoever. You had to ask what the people of Martlesham Heath had done to deserve this brutalism on one side of their village, along with the soaring horror that was the BT research centre spoiling the skyline on the other. I suppose, at the very least, both constructions provided them with jobs.

I went into the reception area and asked to speak with Detective Chief Superintendent Locke. No – I didn't have an appointment. What was it in connection with? The disappearance of Cecily Treherne. The uniformed officer looked doubtful but she made the call while I sat down on one of the plastic chairs provided and leafed through a copy of *Suffolk Life* that was five months out of date. I wasn't sure that Locke would see me, and the officer had given no indication that he had even answered the phone, so I was surprised when after just a few minutes he suddenly appeared, stepping out of a lift. He marched straight over to me with such determination that I wouldn't have been surprised if he had grabbed hold of me, put me under arrest and dragged me into a cell. That was his manner ... always on the edge of violence. It was as if he had caught something, some sort of virus perhaps, from the criminals he investigated. I knew he didn't like me. He'd made that clear the last time we met.

But when he spoke it was almost with amusement. 'Well, well, well. Ms Ryeland. I had a feeling it wasn't coincidence when I clocked you at the hotel. And when they told me you were here, why wasn't I surprised? All right, then. I can give you five minutes. There's an office down here where we can talk ... '

I had done him an injustice. He had noticed me when we passed in the reception area at Branlow Hall. He had just chosen not to acknowledge me. He led me into an empty, soulless room that was perfectly square, with a table and four chairs placed exactly in the middle. A window looked out onto the woodland that surrounded the building. He held the door for me, then closed it as I sat down.

'How are you?' he asked.

The question took me by surprise. 'I'm very well, thank you.'

'I heard what happened when you were here last time, investigating Alan Conway's death. You were almost killed.' He wagged his finger. 'I did warn you not to get involved.'

I couldn't remember him saying anything of the sort but I didn't argue.

'So, what are you doing back in Suffolk and at Branlow Hall? No. You don't need to tell me. I already had Aiden MacNeil on the phone complaining about you. It's funny, isn't it! I'd have said Alan Conway has already caused you enough grief, but you just can't leave him alone.'

'I'd have said he was the one who won't leave me alone, Detective Chief Superintendent.'

'He was a nasty little shit while he was alive and he's still a nasty little shit now that he's dead. Do you really believe he put something in his book? Another secret message ... this time about Frank Parris?'

'Have you read it?' I asked.

'Yes.'

'And?'

Locke stretched out his legs and considered. It struck me that he was being unusually polite, friendly even. But then his argument had always been with Alan Conway, not with me, and with good reason. Alan had asked him for help with his research and in return had turned him into a vaguely comic character – Detective Inspector Raymond Chubb. Chubb and Locke. Get it? He had also created a grotesque parody of Locke's wife who had turned up in the second book, *No Rest for the Wicked*, although I had never met the real woman myself. Perhaps, with Alan's death, Locke had decided to forgive me for my part in all this. It might also have helped that his alter ego didn't make an appearance in *Atticus Pünd Takes the Case*.

'I thought it was the usual load of rubbish,' he said, calmly. 'You know my views on detective fiction.'

'You certainly expressed them very strongly.'

There was no need to remind me but he did. 'Whodun-nits written by the likes of Alan Conway have absolutely no bearing on real life and if the people who read them think otherwise, more fool them. There are no private detectives; not unless you want to spy on your teenage son or find out who your husband is screwing. And murders don't usually take place in thatched cottages or stately homes – or seaside villages, for that matter. *Atticus Pünd Takes the Case*! You tell me one thing in that book – one thing – that isn't complete rubbish. The Hollywood actress who buys a house in the middle of nowhere. That business with the diamond. The knife on the hall table. I mean – please! As soon as you see a knife on a table, you know it's going to end up in some-body's chest.'

'That's what Chekhov said.'

'I'm sorry?'

'The Russian playwright. He said that if you have a pistol on the wall in the first act, then it has to be fired in the second. He was explaining how every element in a story has to have a point.'

'Did he also say that the story has to be unbelievable and the ending completely ridiculous?'

'I take it you didn't guess it, then.'

'I didn't even try. I read the book because I thought it might have something to do with the disappearance of Cecily Treherne and as it turned out that was a total waste of my time.'

'It sold half a million copies worldwide.' I don't know why I was defending Alan Conway. Maybe I was just defending myself.

'Well, you know my thoughts on that, Ms Ryeland. You turn murder into a game and you ask people to join in. What's the police detective called in *Atticus Pünd Takes the Case*? Hare. I suppose he's got that name because he's harebrained. He's a complete idiot, isn't he? Never gets anything right.' He rapped a heavy knuckle on the table. 'You must be very proud of yourself. Half a million copies of infantile crap that trivialises crime and erodes faith in the rule of law.'

'You've made up your mind, but I think you've always been mistaken about crime fiction, Detective Chief Superintendent. Congratulations on the promotion, by the way. I don't think Alan's books ever did anyone any harm – except me. People enjoyed them and they knew perfectly well what they were getting when they read them. Not real life so much as an escape from it – and God knows we're all in need of that right now. Twenty-four-hour news. Fake news. Politicians calling each other liars when they aren't actually lying

150

themselves. Maybe there's something a little comforting in a book that actually makes sense of the world in which it takes place and leads you to an absolute truth.'

He wasn't going to engage with me. 'Why are you here, Ms Ryeland?' he asked.

'If you mean why am I in Martlesham Heath, I was hoping you'd let me see the original police report into Stefan Codrescu. It was eight years ago so it can't be of any interest to anyone now. I'd like to see the forensic reports, the interrogations – all of it.'

He shook his head. 'That's not going to happen.'

'Why not?'

'Because it's confidential! It's police work. You really think we're going to release sensitive information to any member of the public who comes knocking at the door?'

'But suppose Stefan Codrescu didn't do it!'

That was when Locke's patience snapped and his voice took on a threatening tone.

'Listen to me,' he said. 'I was the one who led the investigation, so frankly what you just said is insulting. You weren't anywhere near when the murder happened. You just sat back and let your golden boy turn it into a fairy story. There is absolutely no doubt in my mind that Codrescu killed Frank Parris for the money that he needed to feed his gambling habit. He confessed as much in a room identical to this one just one floor above and his brief was sitting next to him all the time. There were no thumbscrews. No threats.

'Codrescu was a career criminal and it was madness having him in the hotel in the first place. If you're so interested in crime, let me tell you a story – a true story. Just one month before the murder at Branlow Hall, I was part of a team that closed down a Romanian gang operating in Ipswich. They were a charming bunch of people involved in begging, violent assaults and burglary. They were all graduates of a Romanian crime academy. I'm not kidding you. They even had their own textbooks, which taught them how to avoid electronic detection, how to hide their DNA. That sort of thing.

'Well, it turned out that their biggest earner was a brothel in the Ravenswood district and the youngest girl working there was fourteen years old. Fourteen! She'd been trafficked into the country and she was being forced to service three or four men a night. If she refused, they beat her and starved her. Now, is that something you think your readers would enjoy? The continued rape of a fourteen-year-old child? Maybe Atticus Pünd should have been sent out to investigate that one!'

'I don't understand why you're telling me this,' I said. 'Of course it's horrible, what you're describing. But was Stefan Codrescu involved?'

'No . . . ' He stared at me as if I'd missed the point.

'Then what you're saying is, he must have killed Frank Parris because he was Romanian!'

Locke let out something close to a snarl and got to his feet so quickly that his chair would have toppled backwards if it hadn't been screwed to the floor. 'Just get out of here,' he said. 'And get out of Suffolk.'

'Actually, I'm driving to London.'

'That's good. Because if I get the impression that you're obstructing my investigation into the disappearance of Cecily Treherne, I will arrest you.'

I stood up. But I didn't leave yet. 'So what do you think has happened to Cecily?' I asked.

He stared at me. But then he answered. 'I don't know,' he said. 'My guess is that she's dead and that somebody may have killed her. Maybe it was her husband. Maybe they had an argument and he stuck a knife in her, although we haven't found a trace of her DNA on him or anywhere else it shouldn't be. Maybe it was that creepy guy who lives with his mother and works nights. Maybe he had a thing for her. Or maybe it was a complete stranger who just happened to be walking along the River Deben with an erection and a sick mind.

'We may never know. But I'll tell you one thing that it wasn't. It wasn't somebody who was named in a stupid detective story written eight years ago. So get that in your head and go back home. And stop asking questions. I won't warn you again.'

Lawrence Treherne

I stopped at a service station on the edge of London and picked up my emails. Still nothing from Andreas. A confirmation from James Taylor: seven thirty at Le Caprice. And a long note from Lawrence Treherne, which I read over a coffee and a croissant so stale and doughy that it bore no relation to anything you might ever buy in France. The email was very well timed. Here was a step-by-step account of what had happened at Branlow Hall, told from a single perspective. It was interesting to see how it connected with what I already knew. I could also use it as a reference when I met Lionel Corby the next morning.

This is what I read.

*

From: Lawrence Treherne <lawrence.treherne@Branlow.com>
Sent: 21 June 2016 at 14:35
To: Susan Ryeland <S.Ryeland@polydorus.co.gr>
Subject: RE: Cecily

Dear Susan

You asked me about my memories of the wedding day. I'm
writing this with assistance from my wife, although you will
have to forgive the absence of any particular style, which is to
say I am not much of a writer, I'm afraid. The story that Alan
Conway wrote is very different from what happened at Branlow
Hall in 2008 so I do wonder how any of this can be of very
much use to you, but at the same time it can't hurt to have the
facts set out, at least in so far as I remember them.

You might like to know how Aiden and my daughter met and I'll
start there because I believe it is part of the story.

At the start of August 2005, Cecily was in London and she
was thinking of leaving the hotel. As I may have already
mentioned to you, and it pains me to say it, she and her sister
had always had quite a difficult relationship. I don't want you
to read anything into that. Two girls growing up together
are always going to argue about music, clothes, boyfriends
and things like that and my two were no exceptions. Lisa
has always said that Cecily was our favourite but there's no
truth in that. She was our first child and we loved them both
equally.

At the time, the two of them were grown-up and they were
working together at Branlow Hall. The idea was that they would
take it off our hands eventually but the relationship wasn't
working. There was a lot of tension between them and I'm not
going to go into the details as it was nothing more than tittle-

tattle, but the upshot was that Cecily decided to strike out on her own. She'd lived her whole life in Suffolk and she fancied having a crack at the big city. We offered to buy her a flat in London, which may sound extravagant but it was something we had been thinking about already. We liked going down to theatres and concerts and in the long run it would be more economical. So that was why she was there.

She found a place in east London that she liked the look of and Aiden was the estate agent who showed her round. They hit it off immediately. He was a couple of years younger than her but he was doing very well for himself. He'd already saved up enough money to buy himself a place on the Edgware Road, near Marble Arch. Not bad for someone in their twenties, even if it was only one room. While they were talking, Cecily discovered that it was actually his birthday that day and she insisted on going off with him and meeting his friends. That was very much how Cecily behaved. She liked to take the bull by the horns and she told me later that she knew that the two of them were compatible from the very start.

We met Aiden soon after and we liked him very much. As a matter of fact, he did us a huge favour because he was as keen to leave London as Cecily had been to go there and he persuaded her to stay at Branlow Hall. He didn't like the city and he didn't think she would either, but they would keep his flat as a useful bolt-hole if they needed to get away. But as a matter of fact, after he arrived Cecily's relationship with Lisa got a lot better. It was two against one, you see. Aiden gave her self-confidence.

I'm attaching a couple of photographs of Cecily, by the way. You may have seen some of the pictures in the newspapers but none of them did her justice. She's a beautiful girl. She reminds me so much of her mother at that age.

Aiden and Cecily moved into Branlow Cottage six months before they got married. Lisa had been living there but we persuaded her to move into a place we owned in Woodbridge. It made sense, particularly after Roxana was born. Aiden took over the PR side of the business. He did all the brochures, press releases, advertising, special events – and he did a very good job. It was about this time that Pauline and I realised that we could retire with a clear conscience. Lisa was doing a terrific job too. Despite what she said to you the other day, I don't think she disliked Aiden. I rather hoped he'd jolt her into getting married herself.

And so to the point of all this. June 15th 2008. The wedding weekend.

I've gone over every minute of it, starting on the Thursday, and all the problems that came our way. First off there was a bust-up over the phone with the contractors who were supposed to be delivering the marquee. Their lorry had broken down and they were going to be late, which is one of the poorest excuses I'd ever heard. It didn't come in until lunchtime on Friday and it was the devil's own work to get it up on time. Cecily was in a state because one of the bridesmaids had come down with bad flu and she'd managed to lose a pen which I'd lent her. It was a 1956 Montblanc 342 with a gold nib – a really lovely piece, in

157

its original box and never been used. I was actually quite angry with her although I didn't say anything at the time. Anyway, I'd wanted her to have it because it was something old, something new, something borrowed, something blue.

Lisa was always convinced that Stefan must have taken the pen. He was in and out of the house carrying things and it was just sitting there on the table. I mentioned that to the police but it was never found. In the end, Cecily had to make do with two coins, one of Pauline's brooches and a ribbon.

What else? Cecily hadn't slept well all week. Last-minute nerves. I'd given her some diazepam. She didn't want to take it but Aiden and Pauline insisted as we didn't want her going down the aisle looking like a zombie! She needed to look her best and feel her best for the big day. At least we were lucky with the weather. Friday was absolutely glorious. The forecasters getting it right for a change. Our guests started arriving. The marquee finally went up. And we were all able to relax.

I wasn't there when Frank Parris booked in. That was on Thursday afternoon and I was at home in Southwold. I saw him very briefly early on Friday morning when I drove to the hotel. He was getting into a taxi. I caught sight of him wearing a light, fawn-coloured blazer and white trousers. He had curly silver hair, a bit like the boy in that painting by Millais, if you know what I mean. And the thing is I had an idea he was trouble even then. It's easy enough to say it after the event, but he was arguing with the driver who was a regular at the hotel, a very reliable man who was only a couple of minutes late, and I got the sense of a passing cloud. In my view, and I'm not afraid to say it, he and Alan Conway were two of a kind.

We had a party on Friday night. We wanted to thank the staff for all their hard work and of course they would be busy the next day so it seemed only fair. We had it out by the swimming pool. It was a lovely evening, perhaps a little too warm. There was sparkling wine, canapés, Pimm's. Cecily made a speech thanking everyone. It was very much appreciated.

I suppose you'll want to know who was there. Well, basically it was the entire staff, including Anton who was the chef, Lionel, Natasha, William (he looked after the grounds), Cecily, Aiden, Lisa, Pauline and myself and, of course, Stefan. I invited very few of the family, although I seem to remember that Pauline's brother was there. And Aiden's mother, who was very sweet, looked in for about ten minutes before she went to bed. This was meant to be a hotel event rather than part of the wedding. I could send you a complete list if you want it but there were about twenty-five people in all.

I need to tell you about Stefan and I might as well start by saying that despite everything that happened, I always liked him. I found him quiet, hard-working, polite and, at least as far as I could see, grateful for the opportunity we had given him. Cecily was exactly of my mind. As you know, she defended him quite passionately, at least to start with, and she was terribly disappointed when he confessed to the murder. It was only

Lisa who had any doubts about him. She was convinced he was pilfering and it gives me no pleasure at all to acknowledge that in the end she was proved right. I wish now that we'd all listened to her sooner and got rid of Stefan but there's no point going over all that now.

In fact, Lisa and Stefan had met the day before – that was the Thursday – and she had given him his notice. So by the time he came to the pool party on Friday evening, Stefan knew that he was on his way out. We were giving him a generous pay-off – three months' wages – by the way, so he wasn't exactly going to starve, but even so it may well explain what happened consequently. That evening he got quite drunk. Lionel, the spa manager, had to help him back to his room. Maybe he had already decided that he was going to make up for his loss of salary by stealing from the guests. I don't know. I don't know why Lisa had to take the action she did two days before the wedding. It could have been better timed.

One other thing about the party before I move on. Derek Endicott didn't come. He was in a strange mood that evening. I did try to talk to him but he seemed quite distracted, as if he'd had bad news. I should have mentioned this to you before but I'm only remembering it now as I write everything down. Pauline said he looked as if he'd seen a ghost!

Derek was on duty that night. Pauline and I went home at about half past ten. According to the police, Frank Parris was murdered sometime after midnight, attacked with a hammer

160

in room 12, where he was staying. We knew nothing about that until later.

Pauline and I arrived at the hotel the following day, the day of our daughter's wedding, at ten o'clock. We had coffee and biscuits with the guests and the service took place in the rose garden, which is on the south side of the house, on the other side of the ha-ha. It took place at midday with the registrar from Suffolk County Council. Lunch was at twelve forty-five in the marquee with a hundred and ten guests arranged over eight tables. There was a fabulous menu. A Thai cashew and quinoa salad, then poached salmon and then a white peach frangipane galette. I was quite nervous because I had to make a speech and I've never been very comfortable with public speaking, but as things turned out I never said a word. Nobody did.

The moment I became aware that something was wrong was when I heard someone screaming outside the hotel. The sound was muffled by the canvas but it was still clear that something was very wrong. Then Helen came into the tent. Helen was our head of housekeeping. She was a very reliable, quiet woman and nothing would normally ruffle her feathers, but I could see at once that she was very upset. My first thought was that the hotel must be on fire because there was no earthly reason for her to come in otherwise. At first, she wouldn't tell me what was wrong. She asked me to come with her and although the first course was about to be served, I realised I had no choice.

Natasha was waiting outside and she was in a terrible state, as white as a sheet with tears running down her cheeks. She was the one who had found the body and it was an absolutely horrible sight. Frank Parris had been wearing his pyjamas. He was lying on the bed, not in it, with his head smashed in so that he was unrecognisable. There was blood everywhere as well as bits of bone and all the rest of it. Horrible. Helen had already called the police, which was exactly the right thing to do, but of course as you can imagine that signalled an immediate end to the wedding and sure enough, even as we spoke outside the marquee, I heard the first sirens heading our way from the A12.

It's almost impossible to describe what happened next. A perfect English wedding was turned, in a matter of minutes, into a total nightmare. Four police cars turned up in the end and we must have had a dozen or more officers and detectives and photographers and forensics swarming over the grounds. The first person to arrive on the scene was a detective inspector called Jane Cregan and I have to say she did a very good job taking charge. Some of the guests were coming out of the tent wondering what was going on and she made them all go inside and then went in and explained something of what had happened.

She was very sensitive to the situation, but the fact was the party was over and nobody was allowed to leave. One minute they were wedding guests, now they were either suspects or potential witnesses and the marquee had become a giant

holding pen. The ones I felt most sorry for were Aiden and Cecily, of course. They had a room booked in London and a flight leaving the next day for their honeymoon in Antigua.
I talked to Miss Cregan about them being allowed to go. They couldn't have had anything to do with the murder. Neither of them had even met Frank Parris. Well, briefly, the day before. But it didn't make any difference. We got the money back on our insurance in the end and they went to the Caribbean a couple of weeks later, but still, it was hardly a great start to married life.

Part of me still wishes that Natasha hadn't gone into room 12 until later in the day. Maybe Aiden and Cecily could have got away before the body was discovered. Natasha had started work at half past eight and she had gone past room 12 on her way to the Moonflower Wing. At the time, she was sure there had been a 'Do Not Disturb' notice on the door and she had decided to leave it until last. When she went back just after one o'clock, the sign wasn't there. It was actually found in a dustbin further down the corridor. It had been thrown away.

The police did wonder about that. Stefan Codrescu might have placed the sign on the door to disguise what he had done, but when you think about it, there wouldn't have been any point and why would he have taken it off again later? Later on he denied touching it, although the police found his fingerprints on it along with a tiny sample of Frank Parris's blood – so he was obviously lying.

To be honest, it's something I've often thought about and it still makes no sense. The sign was there at half past nine and at one o'clock it was in the bin. What possible explanation can there be? Did someone find the body and feel a need to hide it for three and a half hours? Did Stefan feel a need to go back into the room? In the end, the police decided that Natasha must have got it wrong. Unfortunately, you can't talk to her. She went back to Estonia and I have no idea where she is. I also heard that Helen died a couple of years ago. She had breast cancer. Perhaps DI Cregan can help.

As for Stefan, he had kept a low profile on the day of the wedding. He may have been nursing a hangover, but when I saw him he was sulky and in a bad mood. The toilet off the entrance hall had blocked and he had to deal with it, which wasn't particularly pleasant, but you might as well know that I felt duty-bound to tell the police that he looked as if he'd been awake half the night. His eyes were bleary with lack of sleep. He had a master key to all the rooms and so it would have been easy for him to enter room 12. And he looked exactly like someone who had just committed a horrible crime and was waiting for the axe to fall.

I hope this helps you. I'm still waiting to hear your thoughts on the book. As to your other request, if you would like to give me your partner's bank details, I would be happy to send you an advance on the sum that we agreed. Shall we say £2,500?

Best wishes
Lawrence Treherne

PS The name of the guest we moved out of room 12 was
George Saunders. He had been the headmaster at Bromeswell
Grove secondary school and had come to Suffolk for a
reunion. LT

*

There were two photographs of Cecily attached, both taken
on the day of her wedding.

Lawrence had described his daughter as beautiful and of
course, as her father and on that particular day, what other
word would he use? But it wasn't exactly true. She was wearing an ivory wedding dress with a locket of platinum or white
gold engraved with a heart and an arrow and three stars. Her
naturally blonde hair had been styled immaculately in a way
that made me think of Grace Kelly and she was looking past
the camera as if she had just caught sight of the perfect hap-
piness that lay ahead and that was to be hers. And yet there
was something inescapably ordinary about her. I really don't
want to be cruel. She was an attractive woman. Everything
about the photograph suggested to me that she was some-
body I would like to have known and still hoped, faintly, to
meet.

I suppose all I'm saying is that I could imagine her filling
in her tax forms or doing the washing-up and the gardening, but not speeding round a series of hairpin bends in 1950s
Monaco in an Aston Martin convertible.

I closed my laptop and walked back to the car. I still had
to hit London and then take the North Circular Road all the
way round to Ladbroke Grove. Craig Andrews had said he

165

would be home by four to let me in and I wanted to shower and change clothes before dinner at Le Caprice.

I should have spent longer thinking about what I had read. Lawrence's email contained a great many of the answers to the puzzle. I just hadn't seen them yet.

Ladbroke Grove

When I was working as an editor, I liked to see where my writers lived and worked. I wanted to know what books they had on their shelves and the art they had on their walls, whether their desks were neat and orderly or a battlefield of notes and discarded ideas. It always irritated me that my most successful author, Alan Conway, never once invited me to the sprawling folly that was Abbey Grange (he'd renamed it after a Conan Doyle short story). I only saw it after he was dead.

I'm not sure that we need to know the life story of an author to appreciate his or her work. Take Charles Dickens, for example. Does it add very much to our enjoyment of *Oliver Twist* to know that he had himself been a street urchin in London, working at a blacking factory with a boy who happened to be called Fagin? Conversely, when we meet his female characters is it a distraction to recall how badly he treated his first wife? Literary festivals all over the country turn writers into performers and open doors into their private lives that, I often think, would be better left closed. In my view, it's more satisfying to learn about authors from the work they produce rather than the other way round.

But editing a book is a very different experience from just reading it. It's a collaboration and I always saw it as my job to get inside my writer's head, to share something of the process of creativity. Books may be written in isolation, but their creators are to an extent defined by their surroundings and I always found that the more I knew about them, the more I could help them with what they were trying to achieve.

I'd visited Craig Andrews once when I was editing his first novel. He had a three-bedroom house on a quiet street with residential parking and lots of trees. He had converted the basement into a spacious kitchen and dining area with French windows opening onto a patio. The ground floor was given over to a study/library and a sitting room with a widescreen TV on the wall and an upright piano. The bedrooms were further up on two more floors. Craig had plenty of female friends but he had never been married so the taste was entirely his: expensive but restrained. There were books everywhere, hundreds of them on shelves that had been designed to fit into every nook and cranny, and it goes without saying that anyone who collects books can't be all bad. It might seem strange that someone whose work included graphic descriptions of gang violence and the lengths – or depths – to which women would go to smuggle drugs into jail should have a fondness for romantic poetry and French watercolours, but then it had always been the elegance of his writing – along with its authenticity – that I had admired.

I was the one who had discovered Craig. At least, I had believed the young agent who had recommended him to me and after I had read his manuscript I had snapped him up immediately with a two-book contract. His first novel came with the title *A Life Without Mirrors*, which was actually a rather marvellous quotation from Margaret Atwood: 'To live in prison is to live without mirrors. To live without mirrors is to live without the self.' It was also the first thing I changed. His book was well written but it wasn't literary fiction and Craig certainly wasn't interested in the sort of sales that, unfortunately, go with that territory. *Jail Time* may have been crasser, but it was short and sharp and looked good on the cover. As he'd told me in his email, he'd been doing time ever since.

He greeted me at the door, dressed in his trademark T-shirt and jeans with, I noticed, bare feet. I suppose anyone who has spent twenty years in banking has earned the right to go without a tie or socks. He was forty-four, I remembered from his biography. He looked younger. He belonged to a local gym and he used it. He had the sort of cover photograph that helped sell books.

'Susan! How great to see you.' A kiss on both cheeks. 'Let me help you with that bag. Come on in.'

He showed me up to a comfortable room on the top floor. It was built into the eaves with windows overlooking communal gardens at the back; certainly a step up from the Premier Inn. There was an en-suite bathroom with one of those showers that squirt water in every direction, and Craig suggested I might like to use it and change while he put on the kettle. We would both be out that evening. He was going to the theatre. I had dinner with James Taylor.

'I'll give you a spare set of keys and show you where the fridge is and after that you're on your own.'

It was good to see him again, a reminder of the life I had managed to mislay in the course of my involvement with Alan Conway. I unzipped my wheelie and pulled out my clothes, along with the purchases I'd made in Woodbridge. I'd transferred them to the case when I got out of the car; there was no way I was going to turn up on his doorstep looking as if I'd just been to the sales.

Even so, I was a little uncomfortable as I laid everything out on the bed. Part of it was a feeling I often get when I stay in other people's houses: a sense of crossing a line, of intrusion. It was one of the reasons I had decided against asking Katie to put me up. Had I really come here to save the cost of a couple of nights in a cheap hotel? No. That wasn't fair. Craig had invited me and I hadn't seen any reason not to accept. It would be more pleasant than being on my own.

But I had definitely felt a pang of guilt when I'd called him and now, glancing at my laptop, which was also on the bed, I knew why. I was engaged to Andreas. We might have postponed the wedding but we hadn't completely called it off. The diamond ring was back in the shop, but there were other diamond rings. So what was I doing in the home of a man I barely knew – moreover, a man who was wealthy, single and about my age? I hadn't mentioned any of this to Andreas. What would I have said if he had gone sneaking off to some Athenian lovely? How would I have felt?

Of course, I reminded myself, nothing was going to happen. Craig had never shown any interest in me, or the other way round. But it probably didn't help that even as these thoughts went through my head I was standing in his shower, enjoying, incidentally, the sort of water pressure that we had never been able to achieve in Crete. I felt exposed in every way. I wondered if I should FaceTime Andreas and tell him where I was. At least it would remove any hint of betrayal. I was on business. I was earning ten thousand pounds, which would all go into the hotel. With the time difference, it would be eight o'clock in Crete, dinner time for the guests even though the locals preferred to eat much later. Andreas might be helping out in the kitchen. He might be looking after the bar. He must have read my email by now! Why hadn't he FaceTimed me?

The laptop was still sitting there accusingly when I came out. I decided to give it another day before I emailed him again. Craig was waiting for me downstairs and it would be rude to keep him waiting too long. And maybe I didn't want to talk to Andreas. He was the one who needed to talk to me.

I put on the new cocktail dress and a pair of simple silver earrings I'd bought myself in Crete. A final dash of perfume on each wrist and I went downstairs.

'You look great.' Craig flicked off the kettle as I came into the kitchen and poured boiling water into a glass teapot with big, authentic-looking leaves. He had also changed into a long-sleeved shirt. And he had socks as well as shoes. 'It's white tea from Sri Lanka,' he continued. 'I was at the Galle festival last February.'

'How was it?'

'Wonderful. Except that any writers who upset them, they tend to throw in jail. I shouldn't have gone.' He brought two cups and saucers over to the table. 'And on the subject of jail, did you write to Stefan Codrescu?'

'I'm still waiting to hear from him.'

'So what's that about?'

171

I told him about the book that Alan had written, about Lawrence and Pauline Treherne and their visit to Crete, about Cecily's disappearance. I did my best to make it sound less like an adventure with me as the plucky heroine on the trail of a killer. Maybe I was thinking of what Richard Locke had said to me in Martlesham Heath. Cecily Treherne, a mother with a young child, could have been murdered while she was out walking her dog. There was no doubt that Frank Parris had been beaten to death eight years before. It was all too easy to trivialise these two events, to make them sound merely entertaining. That wasn't why I was here. I wasn't Atticus Pünd. My job, I explained, was to read the book and to see if I could find in it anything that might help.

'How well did you know Alan Conway?' Craig asked.

'Well, I published his first novel, the same as yours,' I said. 'You were a lot nicer, though.'

Craig smiled. 'Thanks.'

'I mean it. In the end I worked on nine of his novels and I loved them ... at least until I got to the end.'

'Are you going to tell me what happened?'

I had no choice. After all, I had accepted his hospitality. I told him everything, aware of the passing of time only from the fact that at some stage we moved on from white tea to white wine.

'That's an extraordinary story,' he said, when I had finally finished. 'Do you mind if I ask you something?'

'Go ahead.'

'You nearly got yourself killed while you were investigating. And now you're doing it a second time? You're suggesting that someone may have murdered Cecily because of what she knew. Couldn't the same thing happen to you?'

Katie had said exactly the same thing and I gave him the same reply. 'I'm being careful.'

But was it true? I'd had meetings with Aiden MacNeil, with Derek Endicott, with Lisa Treherne and with Martin and Joanne Williams. I'd been on my own with them and any one of them could have been lying to me. Any one of them could have beaten a man to death with a hammer. The nanny was creepy and even the detective was vaguely threatening. These certainly weren't the sort of people I should be mixing with, but how could I get anything out of them without trusting them, at least to some extent? Maybe I was putting myself in danger after all.

'Have you reread the book?' Craig asked.

'*Atticus Pünd Takes the Case?* Not yet. I thought I'd start it on Monday.'

'Here – you can have my copy if you like.' He went over to a bookshelf and returned with the new edition in his hand. 'Someone bought it for me, but I've still got the old edition upstairs. Unless you've already got one ... ?'

'No. I was going to buy it.'

'Then that'll save you.' He looked at his watch. 'I have to go,' he said. 'I may not see you later. The play doesn't finish until half ten.'

'Why don't you let me buy you dinner tomorrow night? I haven't asked you anything about your writing or your new publishers and all the rest of it. I take it you're not married or anything?'

'Good God, no!'

'Then let's go somewhere local. If you don't mind me staying a second night.'

'Not at all. I'd like that.'

He left ahead of me and it was only after he had gone that I realised what should have been obvious from the start. With his neat beard, his dark skin and his brown eyes, Craig reminded me very much of Andreas, several years younger and wealthier – in every respect in better shape. The thought was an unworthy one but it was true. I've always been attracted to a certain type of man and it occurred to me that if Andreas was the reality, Craig was the ideal.

But I was with Andreas.

I took an Uber into town. There would have been nowhere to park my MG so I'd left it in a car park near Ladbroke Grove station. It took me half an hour to get to Le Caprice.

And all the way I thought of Craig.

Le Caprice, London

The last time I'd had dinner with James Taylor, the two of us had got very drunk together and I was determined it wasn't going to happen again – certainly not at the sorts of prices you pay at Le Caprice. I'd only ever been there once – Charles Clover, my boss, took me for my birthday and that wasn't a relationship that had ended well. The food was great, but what I remember was everyone staring at me as I crossed the room. It's impossible to reach your table without being seen, which may be the point for half the people who eat there but it doesn't work for me. I prefer places that are more anonymous, where I don't feel I have to be on my best behaviour. I wondered why James had chosen it. It was certainly a step up from the Crown in Framlingham.

He was ten minutes late and I was beginning to think he was going to stand me up when he came bounding in, shown to our table by a waiter who seemed to know him well. It was two years since I had seen him and as he crossed the room I thought he looked exactly the same. The long hair, the baby face with its contradictory stubble, the eyes full of enjoyment and enthusiasm, though with just a hint of something sly around the corner ... I had taken an immediate liking to him when we'd first met at Abbey Grange and hoped I would feel the same now.

But as he sat down, apologising about the traffic, I saw that something wasn't quite right, that he looked tired, strained. He had been partying too late, drinking too much and possibly taking too many drugs – he had the classic looks of a sybarite, and if there was something Byronesque about him, I had to remind myself that Lord Byron was dead, killed by sepsis, at just thirty-six. He was dressed in the same black leather jacket and T-shirt that he had always favoured, although the brands were more expensive. As he raised a hand to order champagne, I noticed a gold bracelet and two rings that hadn't been there before.

'Susan, it was such a surprise to hear from you! Dinner's on me and I won't hear of any argument. How are you? I heard you got hurt when you were trying to find out who killed Alan. That's awful! It's hard to believe that he was actually murdered. I wonder what he would have thought of that! It probably helped sell the books.'

I relaxed. His appearance might have changed but James was still very much his old self. 'I don't think he'd have been too impressed,' I said. 'He didn't much like murder stories.'

'He'd have liked being in the newspapers. We often used to talk about how many inches he'd get. In his obituary, I mean!' He hooted with laughter, then grabbed the menu. 'I'm going to have scallops and steak and chips. I love the food here. And I want to hear everything that happened. Why was

Alan killed, exactly? Who had he upset? And how did you get involved?'

'I'll tell you everything,' I said, thinking that I'd already gone through it all with Craig and was beginning to feel fed up with the whole thing. 'But first I want to hear about you and how you've been getting on. Are you acting in anything? The last time we met, you said you were going back to drama school.'

'I did apply to RADA and Central but they weren't interested in me. I'm probably too old and debauched. Anyway, my heart isn't really in it and I've got so much money now I don't need to work. Did you know that we sold Abbey Grange for two million quid? I don't know who'd pay that much to sit in a field in the middle of sodding Suffolk, but I'm not complaining. Alan's books are still selling and they keep sending me royalty cheques. It's like winning the lottery except it happens every six months.'

Alan Conway had been married. He'd had a child with his wife, Melissa, but six months after the publication of *Atticus Pünd Takes the Case*, he had come out as gay, the two of them had divorced and eventually she'd moved to Bradford-on-Avon in Wiltshire. For at least one year during their relationship, Alan had taken to using rent boys. He'd picked them up in London in the early days of the Internet, when cards in telephone boxes were slowly being phased out. My dinner companion had been one of them.

James had spared no details telling me about their time together – the sex, the surreptitious travel to France and the USA. I'd actually found his shamelessness quite endearing. Alan had employed James as his 'researcher' and I'm sure all the money he was paying – effectively for sex – he had claimed as a tax-deductible expense. After the divorce, James had moved in with him, although the twenty-year age gap hadn't made things easy for either of them. James Fraser, who turned up in the fourth novel as Pünd's sidekick, was based on him; a slightly kinder portrait than the one Conway had inflicted on me. He had appeared in every book until the end.

We ordered our food. The champagne arrived and James told me about his new life in London. He had bought himself a flat in Kensington, which was where he had been living before. He travelled a lot. He'd had a series of affairs but now he was in a serious relationship with an older man, a jewellery designer. 'He's a bit like Alan, really. It's funny how you always end up going back for more of the same.' His partner, Ian, was encouraging him to settle down, to do something with his life, but he couldn't decide what.

'Did you know they're making the TV series of the first Atticus Pünd?' he told me.

'When do they start shooting?'

'They already have. They've got Sir Kenneth Branagh playing Atticus Pünd and I'm an executive producer!' He beamed with pleasure. 'I'm not in the first book, but if they make all of them, someone will end up playing me. I've suggested Ben Whishaw. What do you think?'

After the first course – and the food was delicious – I reluctantly steered the conversation back to Alan Conway. It was, after all, the whole point of the meeting. That meant giving him a quick rundown of everything that had happened since Crete. He had read about Cecily Treherne's disappearance in the papers but it hadn't made much of an impression on him. He was much more interested in Alan's involvement in the original murder and when I told him the name of the victim, he took me completely by surprise.

'I knew Frank Parris,' he said.

'How?'

'How do you think, darling? He fucked me ... quite a few times, as I recall.'

The tables at Le Caprice are quite close together and I noticed the couple eating next to us turn their heads.

'Where?'

'In London! He had a flat in Shepherd Market – not far from here, actually. I never liked having clients in my own space. I usually went to hotels. Nice and anonymous. But Frank wasn't in the closet. Far from it! He'd take you to restaurants and clubs and show you off to his friends before he took you home.'

'Why did he use rent boys?'

'Because he could! Frank had a taste for young boys and he could afford to pay for them. He wasn't into marriage and partners and all that ... or maybe he was but he never admitted it. Anyway, he was quite kinky. It might not have been easy to find a partner who wanted to do the sort of things he liked.'

'What sort of things?'

The words had slipped out before I could stop them but James wasn't embarrassed. 'Humiliation, mainly. Dressing up. A bit of bondage. I met quite a few men like that. Out to give you a bad time ... '

The people at the next table were listening with interest.

179

'How did Alan meet him?' I asked, deliberately lowering my voice and hoping he would do the same.

'I don't know exactly but it wouldn't have been difficult. There were plenty of bars in London, or it could have been in one of those Chariots places. You know — a bathhouse. We actually had a foursome once — me and Alan and Frank and Leo. I'm talking about dinner, by the way! Not what you think! I got the impression that Frank was Alan's spirit guide, if you like. Alan was still very unsure of himself, his sexuality, and Frank encouraged him along the way.'

'Who was Leo?'

'Another rent boy. Like me.' James still hadn't lowered his voice and I was aware of a certain hush at the other tables around us. I'm sure this wasn't the usual sort of conversation you'd hear at Le Caprice. 'A lot of us knew each other,' he went on. 'We didn't exactly socialise, but it helped to know if there were any weirdos out there … pretty policemen, that sort of thing.'

'Were you living with Alan at the time Frank was murdered?'

'No. Not yet. Although we were seeing quite a bit of each other and Alan was already talking about us moving in together. We were actually away when it happened. We heard the news on the radio.' He thought back. 'I have to say, I was quite shocked. I mean, if Frank had been hammered to death in his London flat or in a backstreet in Soho, you wouldn't have blinked. It would have just gone with the territory — particularly with his predilections. But in a posh hotel in the middle of the country … !'

'Was Alan upset?'

That was more difficult to answer. 'I wouldn't say he was upset. No. But he was intrigued. He was on a book tour in Europe. You probably remember. Alan hated touring. That was the funny thing about him. He hated the people who loved his books. We were in France and Holland and Germany, and after it was all over he rented a villa in Tuscany for three weeks, up in the hills. It was a beautiful place.'

'So when did he hear about the death?'

'I heard about it on the radio and I told him. Anyway, he went round to the hotel almost as soon as we got back – not because he gave a toss about Frank Parris, but because he thought he might be able to use it in his next book.'

The second course came. Steak for James, Dover sole for me. As I watched the waiter expertly slicing away with two knives, it occurred to me that in a way he and I were doing exactly the same thing: separating the flesh to find the bones underneath. The only difference was that he would discard them. I needed them to make sense of what had happened.

'The thing is that Alan was stuck,' James went on. 'He was in a foul mood in Tuscany. The first two books had done brilliantly. He was already well known and the money was pouring in. Well, of course, you'd know that, wouldn't you. It was mainly thanks to you. But the third book wouldn't come.'

'Not until he visited Branlow Hall.'

'That's right. He actually took a room and stayed there a couple of nights, although there was hardly any need as he only lived twenty minutes away and he was quite nervous he was going to run into Melissa.'

'Why?' I was puzzled. 'I thought she'd moved to Bradford-on-Avon.'

'No. That was later. After they split up and sold their house in Orford, she wanted to stay close for a while. I don't know why. Maybe she just needed time to work things out. So she rented a house that was actually right next to the hotel. In fact, there was a gate at the bottom of her garden and it led into the grounds.'

So Melissa had been on the scene too! I filed the information away for later.

'That never happened, thank goodness,' James went on. 'You have to remember that she knew he was gay but nobody else did. He hadn't come out yet and he hadn't told anyone about me! Did you know about him?'

'No! I only found out when I read about it in the newspapers.'

'Well, that was Alan for you. Anyway, he spent three or four days there and I knew he'd got the story for his book because when he came back he was in a great mood and he said he'd spoken to loads of people and knew what he was going to write.'

My ears pricked up at that. 'Do you know who he spoke to?'

'Everyone!' When James had come in, he had been carrying a plastic shopping bag that he had dumped on the floor, under the table. Now he picked it up and showed it to me. 'I've brought everything I could find. There are photographs, notes, memory sticks ... some of them with recordings. There may be more stuff at the house. If I find anything else, I'll let you know.'

'That's fantastic, James. Thank you.' I was actually very surprised. 'I didn't think you'd have kept his old papers.'

James nodded. 'I wasn't going to,' he said. 'When I sold the house I was going to chuck it all out. You have no idea how much of it there was. For a start there were hundreds of books. Nine titles in thirty languages!'

'Thirty-four,' I corrected him.

'What was I going to do with Atticus Pünd in Japanese? And then there were the manuscripts, the proof copies, the notepads, all the different drafts. I actually had someone coming in a van from Ipswich to take it all to the local dump. But then two things happened. First of all, I got a call from some university in America. They said they were very sorry to hear of Alan's death and that they were interested in ac-quiring his archive. Note the word "acquiring"! They didn't say they would pay, at least not in so many words, but they did make it clear that all his old manuscripts and all the rest of it had a value.

'And then – this was before probate came through and I was very short of cash – I decided to sell some of Alan's books. I chose some of his Agatha Christies. He had the whole lot, you know. So I took a handful into a second-hand bookshop in Felixstowe and I was very lucky that the owner was honest because he told me that they were all first edi-tions and they were worth a small fortune! The one about Roger Ackroyd was worth two thousand on its own. And there was me expecting to get enough money for fish and chips ... and I'm not talking about the sort of fish and chips you get here!'

'So you've still got everything,' I said.

'I've told the university to make an offer. I'm still waiting. But I kept everything else – the whole lot of it! I was meaning to go through it all and work out what was what, but I'm a lazy bastard and I still haven't got round to it. Anyway, after you rang, I pulled out everything I could find relating to *Atticus Pünd Takes the Case*. That was the right book, wasn't it?'

'Yes.'

'You're lucky that everything is labelled. Alan was like that. If anyone wrote anything about him in the newspapers, he cut it out and stuck it in a book. He was quite an expert on himself.' He laughed gleefully. 'I'd like to have it all back, if you don't mind. You might be looking at my old age pension.'

It was hard to imagine James Taylor ever being old.

'Did he talk to you about the murder?'

'Alan never talked to me about his books, even when he put me in them. But, like I say, he was in a much better mood when he came home and I'll tell you one thing he did say: "*They've got the wrong man*." He was quite smug about it.'

'He was talking about Stefan Codrescu.'

'I don't know who that is.'

'He was the man who was arrested.'

'Well, I think that's exactly what Alan meant. He actually knew the detective in charge of the investigation and he was quite convinced he'd ballsed it all up.'

'But he didn't tell you who the killer was.'

'No. I'm sorry.'

'You'd have thought if he really knew who murdered Frank Parris, he'd have said. Especially since Frank was his friend.'

James grimaced. 'That's not necessarily true. I was fond of Alan, but he could be a complete tosser. He was one of the most selfish men I've ever met. I don't think he gave a damn about Frank Parris or whoever killed him.' He prodded his fork in my direction. 'Anyway, it's quite possible he didn't know. Do you?'

'No,' I admitted.

'But you'll find out.' He smiled. 'I must say, Susan, it is funny the two of us here, together again. And the ghost of Alan still hovering over us. I wonder if he'll ever leave us alone?' He picked up his glass. 'To Alan!'

We clinked glasses.

But I didn't drink.

Cecily Treherne

It was late when I got back to Ladbroke Grove but there was no way I was going to sleep. I upended the plastic bag that James had given me and allowed the contents to spill out onto the bed. There was a full typescript of *Atticus Pünd Takes the Case* with annotations in the margins, the whole thing bound in a plastic cover, several notebooks, half a dozen photographs, some drawings, newspaper clippings about the murder at Branlow Hall, including the pieces from the *East Anglian Daily Times* I had already read, various computer printouts and three memory sticks. Looking at this collection, I was quite certain that the answers I was looking for must be in front of me. Who had killed Frank Parris and where was Cecily Treherne? This was evidence that even the police hadn't seen. But where was I to begin?

The manuscript was, as far as I could see, a second draft and it might have been of interest to a keen-eyed archivist. For example, the first sentence of the book originally read: *Tawleigh-on-the-Water was a tiny village that consisted*

of little more than a harbour and two narrow streets surround-
ed by no fewer than four different stretches of water. Alan had
circled three words, *tiny*, *little* and *narrow*, and I would have
done the same. There are just too many descriptions relating
to smallness in one sentence. He then crossed out the whole
paragraph and used it later on in the first chapter, opening it
instead in the kitchen of Clarence Keep, or Clarence Court,
as it was originally called.

And so on. There was nothing here that would have been
of any interest to the world at large and it certainly had no
relevance to the murder.

The notebooks were similarly academic. I recognised
Alan's neat, cramped handwriting, the pale blue ink that he
favoured. There were dozens of pages filled with questions,
ideas, crossings-out, arrows.

Algernon knows about will.
Blackmails him?
Jason had one-night stand with Nancy.
£60
Knickers stolen from drawer.

Some of the names would change but most of these ideas
would turn up in one form or another. He had drawn detailed
floor plans of Branlow Hall, which he had used as the basis of
the Moonflower Hotel in his book, simply lifting it up brick
by brick and depositing it in Devon. As with all of his books,
the village where the crime takes place does not really exist,
but looking at the maps, he seemed to have imagined it somewhere just down the coast from Appledore.

The computer printouts mainly came from the writer's best friend, Wikipedia, and included articles about famous diamonds, cinema in the UK, the growth of St-Tropez, the Homicide Act of 21 March 1957, and other plot strands that I recognised from the novel.

One of the memory sticks contained images of the people he had met. I recognised Lawrence and Pauline Treherne, Lisa and Cecily, Aiden MacNeil and Derek. Another picture showed a short, stocky woman with cropped hair and narrow eyes wearing a black dress and a white apron. I assumed this must be Natasha Mälk, the Estonian maid who had found the body. Another man – possibly Lionel Corby – had been snapped posing outside the spa. There were also pictures of the building: room 12, the stable block, the bar, the lawn where the wedding had taken place. It gave me an uneasy feeling to recognise that, from the very start, I had been following in his footsteps.

James had added one old-fashioned photograph, actually printed on paper, and it caught my eye at once because Alan was in it. He was sitting between two people in what looked like an expensive restaurant, possibly in London. A very much younger James was on one side. A man with curly grey hair and a deep suntan, dressed in a velvet jacket, was on the other. This had to be Frank Parris. Had James been with Frank or with Alan that night? It was hard to be sure. The three of them were close together, smiling.

I had assumed that the picture must have been taken by a waiter, but looking at it more closely, I realised that the camera was too low and too close. The table was laid for four and it was being held by the fourth member of the group. Could this have been Leo, the rent boy James had mentioned? Two men and two boys. It seemed quite possible.

Downstairs, I heard the front door open and close. Craig had got back from the theatre. I had only put on one bedside lamp and had drawn the curtains before I sat down, and it was when I found myself staying quite still and holding my breath that I realised I had done all this quite deliberately, so that no light would escape and there was no chance that I would be disturbed. I waited as Craig climbed the stairs. I heard a second door open and close. I let out a breath.

I turned my attention to the other memory sticks. I plugged the second one into my laptop. It contained interviews with Lawrence, with Pauline and with Lisa. Those weren't the ones I was interested in, not right now. I took the last one and plugged it in. And there it was – exactly what I had hoped for.

Cecily Treherne.

I'd brought headphones and, feeling quite nervous, I plugged them in. I didn't know if Cecily was dead or alive, but she was the reason I was here and I had felt her ghost hovering over me from the moment I had arrived in Suffolk. Did I actually want to hear her voice? There was something quite macabre in the thought that this might be all that re-mained of her. For that matter, it had been quite a few years since I had heard Alan Conway and I certainly had no desire to commune with him beyond the grave. But this was the in-terview I most needed to hear. There was no way I was going to wait until the morning.

I moved the cursor and hit PLAY.

There was a brief pause and then I heard them. It was a shame that video cameras wouldn't be introduced into smart phones for another few years because I would have loved to have seen them too. What was Cecily wearing? What did she look like, even, when she moved? And where were they? Somewhere inside the hotel from the sounds of it, but it was impossible to be sure.

Alan was on his best behaviour. I almost smiled, recognising the slightly smarmy quality to his voice. He could be ingratiating when he wanted to be, as I knew from experience, although in my case it had always been followed by a series of complaints or an unreasonable demand. It didn't bother me that I couldn't see him. Nearly all of my conversations with him had been over the telephone and this was how I knew him. With Cecily it was different. For the first time, she had half come to life – though only half. She had a similar voice to her sister, Lisa. She sounded like a nice person, warm and relaxed.

It was hard to believe that the conversation had taken place eight years ago. The voices were perfectly preserved and it suddenly struck me that when my parents died, the first memory that I'd lost had been what they sounded like. That would never happen again. Modern technology has changed the nature of death.

ALAN: Hello, Mrs MacNeil. Thank you for talking to me.
CECILY: I'm still not used to being called that. Please, call me Cecily.
ALAN: Ah yes. Of course. How was the honeymoon?
CECILY: Well, obviously it was quite difficult, at first, after what happened. It was two weeks late. But we stayed at a lovely hotel. Have you ever been to Antigua?

ALAN: No.

CECILY: Nelson's Bay. We both needed a holiday, that's for sure.

ALAN: Well, you've managed to get a fantastic tan.

CECILY: Thank you.

ALAN: I don't want to take up too much of your time.

CECILY: That's OK. Everything's very quiet today. How's
          your room?

ALAN: It's very nice. This is a lovely hotel.

CECILY: Yes.

ALAN: By the way, did you know that my ex-wife is renting a
          property from you?

CECILY: Which property?

ALAN: Oaklands.

CECILY: Melissa! I didn't know the two of you ...

ALAN: We separated last year.

CECILY: Oh. I'm sorry. We've chatted once or twice.
          I sometimes see her in the spa.

ALAN: Don't worry. It was all very amicable and I'm just glad
          that she's happy here. I hope it doesn't upset you,
          talking about what happened.

CECILY: No. It's been more than a month now and we've had
          room twelve cleaned out. A lot of bad things happen
          in hotels ... it's like in that film, The Shining. I don't
          know if you ever saw it? I hardly met Frank Parris and
          fortunately I didn't see into the room, so it doesn't
          bother me too much. I'm sorry. I don't mean to be
          dismissive. I know he was your friend.

ALAN: I hadn't seen him for a while. We met in London.

CECILY: And you live in Framlingham now?

ALAN: Yes.

CECILY: Aiden tells me you're a writer.

ALAN: Yes. I've had two books published. *Atticus Pünd
           Investigates* and *No Rest for the Wicked*.

CECILY: I'm afraid I haven't read them. I never have time to
           read very much.

ALAN: They've done quite well.

CECILY: Are you going to write about us?

ALAN: That's not my plan. As I explained to your parents, I
           just want to know what happened. Frank was very
           kind to me when I was trying to work things out and
           I feel I owe it to him.

CECILY: I'd just feel very uncomfortable being in a book.

ALAN: I never put people in my books and certainly not
           without their permission. And I don't write true crime.

CECILY: Well, I suppose that's all right, then.

ALAN: Anyway, I understand the police have made an arrest.

CECILY: Stefan. Yes.

ALAN: Can you tell me about him?

CECILY: What do you want to know?

ALAN: Were you surprised when they arrested him?

CECILY: Yes, I was. Very. In fact, I was shocked. You know my
           parents have always employed young offenders at
           the hotel and I think it's a wonderful idea. We have
           to help these people. I know Stefan had been in
           trouble but that wasn't his fault. He never really had
           a chance when you think about the world he grew up
           in. But once he came to the hotel, he was always very
           grateful, he worked hard and I think he was kind-
           hearted. I know my sister didn't like him, but that
           was because he wouldn't do what she wanted.

192

ALAN: And what was that?

CECILY: I mean, he didn't work hard enough. That's what she said. She also thought he was stealing, but that could have been anyone. It could have been Lionel or Natasha or anyone. She only picked on him because she knew I liked him and I thought it was wrong to fire him. I wouldn't tell you this if I hadn't said exactly the same to her. She didn't have any proof. I think it was unfair.

ALAN: The police think he may have broken into Frank's room because he had been fired ... because he knew he was leaving the hotel.

CECILY: That's what they said, but I'm not sure it's true.

ALAN: You don't think he did it?

CECILY: I don't know, Mr Conway. I didn't think so to begin with. I talked about it with Aiden and even he agreed with me, even though he'd never been one of Stefan's greatest fans. Stefan was one of the gentlest people I'd ever met. He was always very proper in his dealings with me. And like I said, he knew my parents had given him a real opportunity having him here and he would never have let them down. When I heard he'd confessed, I couldn't believe it. And now the police are saying that they've got more than enough evidence to prosecute, although they won't tell me what it is. I don't know. They seem to think it's an open-and-shut case. They say they found money in his room ... I'm sorry. Can you excuse me a moment? It's just that it's all so horrible and upsetting ... someone getting killed.

193

The recording is turned off, then turned on again.

CECILY: I'm sorry.

ALAN: No. I can understand. It was your wedding day. The whole thing must have been awful for you.

CECILY: It was.

ALAN: We can do this later, if you like.

CECILY: No. Let's do it now.

ALAN: Well, I was wondering if you could tell me more about Frank Parris.

CECILY: I didn't see very much of him. I told you.

ALAN: Did you see him on the Thursday he arrived?

CECILY: No. I heard he didn't like his room – but Aiden dealt with that. Aiden's brilliant with the guests. Everyone seems to like him and if there's ever any problems, he always finds a way round them.

ALAN: He moved Frank into room twelve.

CECILY: He swapped him with another guest. A teacher or something. He hadn't arrived yet so he wouldn't know.

ALAN: And then on Friday he went in a taxi to Westleton.

CECILY: Derek arranged that for him. Have you spoken to Derek?

ALAN: Your night manager? I'm seeing him this evening.

CECILY: I saw Mr Parris around lunchtime when he got back. I was having to deal with the people about the marquee. They'd actually let us down quite badly – we won't use them again – by arriving late. It was all right in the end but I was out on the east lawn when he came back in another taxi and Aiden came out at that moment and I saw the two of them chatting.

ALAN: Do you know what they were talking about?

CECILY: Oh – just the hotel, the room, that sort of thing. I wanted to see Aiden so I went over and joined them. He introduced me.

ALAN: What did you make of Frank Parris?

CECILY: Can I be honest? I know he was your friend and I don't want to offend you.

ALAN: Please. You can say what you like.

CECILY: Well, I didn't really take to him. It's difficult to explain and part of it may be that I had my mind on other things. But I found him quite … I didn't believe him. I thought he was being just too friendly and pleasant – he was all over Aiden for changing his room – but all the time I got the feeling that he was just pretending. When he said he loved the hotel I got the feeling that he didn't really like it at all. And when he congratulated Aiden and me because we were getting married, it was almost as if he was sneering at us.

ALAN: Frank could be a little bit … supercilious.

CECILY: I'm not even sure I know what that means.

ALAN: Condescending.

CECILY: It was more than that. He was lying. And actually, I can give you an example. Aiden said that we were having a party that night to celebrate the wedding and he hoped the noise wouldn't disturb him. And Frank said it didn't matter because he was out that evening. He was going to Snape Maltings to see a

performance of *The Marriage of Figaro*. I don't know
anything about opera, but I remember that he was
absolutely specific about the name. He went on
and on about how it was his favourite opera and
he'd always enjoyed it and that he couldn't wait to
see it.

ALAN: What makes you think he was lying?

CECILY: I know he was lying because I happened to go to
          Snape Maltings a couple of days later – they had a
          market – and I saw a list of all the events and *The
          Marriage of Figaro* wasn't on it. They had a youth
          orchestra playing Benjamin Britten that Friday night.

ALAN: Why do you think he would make up something
          like that?

CECILY: Because of what I just told you. He was sneering
          at us.

ALAN: It still seems quite a strange thing to do.

CECILY: I don't think there was any reason for it. I just think
          he enjoyed being superior. Maybe it was because he
          was gay and we were straight. Is that a bad thing to
          say? He'd lived in London and we were stuck out in
          the country. He was the guest and we were just the
          staff. I don't know. When he said goodbye to us, he
          had this weird handshake. He sort of took Aiden's
          hand in both of his like he was the president or
          something and didn't want to let him go. And then
          he gave me a kiss, which I didn't think was at all
          appropriate, and at the same time he had his hand
          very low on my back. I don't know why I'm telling you
          all this. All I'm saying is, he was playing with us. I only

196

met him for a few minutes and you knew him a lot better than me, but I didn't think he was a nice man. I'm sorry, but that's the truth.

ALAN: Did you see him again?

CECILY: No. I had the party on Friday night and I didn't even think about him. The hotel was full anyway, so there were plenty of other guests to worry about. I went to bed early with a sleeping pill and of course the next day was my wedding.

ALAN: Did you see Stefan Codrescu at the party?

CECILY: Yes. He was there.

ALAN: How was he?

CECILY: Well, obviously Lisa had just fired him so he wasn't very happy. In fact, he hardly said anything. Aiden said he'd had too much to drink. He left quite early. I think Lionel took him back to his room.

ALAN: But a few hours later he was up again. According to the police that's when he went back into the hotel, into room twelve.

CECILY: That's what they said.

ALAN: Derek saw him.

CECILY: He might have been wrong.

ALAN: You think so?

CECILY: I don't know. I can't talk to you about all that. Actually, if you haven't got any other questions, I think I've told you everything I know.

ALAN: You've been very helpful, Cecily. And that is a great tan. How are you enjoying married life?

CECILY: (*Laughs.*) Well, it's early days. But we had a wonderful time in Antigua and now I'm glad to be back. We're very happy in Branlow Cottage and I just want to put everything behind us and get on with it.

ALAN: Thank you very much.

CECILY: Thank you.

The recording ended and there was something quite oppressive about the silence that followed. It reminded me that she was still missing after ten days and I wondered if anyone would ever hear her voice again.

There was another interview on the memory stick. Aiden had told me that he had met Alan briefly. I had to play it a couple of times before I realised that this must have happened before Alan spoke to Cecily. The two men were introduced by Pauline Treherne and Alan was already recording.

PAULINE: I'm sorry. I don't really want to be recorded.

ALAN: It's just for my private use. Easier than taking notes.

PAULINE: Even so, I don't feel comfortable about what happened. You're sure you're not going to write about it?

ALAN: No, no. My new book doesn't even take place in Suffolk.

PAULINE: Do you have a title for it?

ALAN: Not yet.

Aiden arrives.

PAULINE: This is Aiden MacNeil. My son-in-law.

ALAN: We've already met, I think.

AIDEN   Yes. I was in reception when you arrived. I helped you change rooms. I hope you're more comfortable now.

ALAN: It's fine, thank you very much.

AIDEN: Excuse me, are you recording this?

ALAN: Yes, I am. Do you mind?

AIDEN: As a matter of fact, I do.

PAULINE: Mr Conway is asking questions about the murder.

AIDEN: Well, I'd prefer not to talk about it.

ALAN: I'm sorry ... ?

AIDEN: Forgive me, Mr Conway. My whole job here is to look after the interests of the hotel. This business with Stefan Codrescu has been nothing but trouble for us and I really don't think we need any more publicity.

ALAN: I'm not going to share these tapes with anyone.

AIDEN: Even so. We told the police everything that happened that day. We didn't hide anything. And if you're going to suggest that the hotel was in some way responsible ...

ALAN: That isn't my intention.

AIDEN: We can't be sure of that.

PAULINE: Aiden ... !

AIDEN: I'm sorry, Pauline. I already told Lawrence that I think this is a bad idea. I'm sure Mr Conway is a very respected writer—

ALAN: Please, call me Alan ...

AIDEN: I'm not playing this game. I'm sorry. Do you mind turning that off?

ALAN: If you insist.

AIDEN: I do.

And that was the end of it.

It was obvious that Aiden had disliked Alan Conway from the moment they met – and I could understand that. Should I read something into the fact that he had refused to be interviewed? No. As Aiden had clearly said, he was only doing his job.

It was after midnight and I had an early start, but the last thing I did before I went to bed was go to Apple Music and download *The Marriage of Figaro*. I would listen to it the next day.

Lionel Corby (Breakfast)

I was tired the next morning. I hadn't slept well and I left the house at first light, before Craig had even got up. I had to cross the whole of London for my 7 a.m. meeting with Lionel Corby, the spa manager who had been working at Branlow Hall at the time of the murder, and I sat bleary-eyed on the Tube for what felt like an eternity, glancing through a free newspaper that only had enough material for two or three stops.

My first impression of Lionel Corby wasn't a very favourable one. He came weaving through the traffic on one of those very expensive bikes with ultra-thin wheels, wearing Lycra that stopped halfway down his thigh and which had clearly been designed to show off his perfect musculature and, for that matter, his well-formed genitalia. I like to think the best of people, a trait not entirely helpful when investigating a murder perhaps, but there was something about him that instantly struck me as . . . well, cocky. Yes, he worked in a gym. He had to advertise his physique, but did he have to do it so loudly? As we shook hands, his eyes travelled over me and I felt positively dowdy. By contrast, he crooned over the bicycle as he chained it to the rack.

'So, Susan, are you going to have some breakfast?' He had one of those exaggerated, sing-song Australian accents. 'They've got a decent café and I get a discount.'

We went inside. Virgin Active occupied a concrete bunker on a busy main road. Curiously, Atticus Pünd had lived in a flat just round the corner ... which is to say, Alan Conway had used the building as his inspiration. The café had only just opened and there was no one else there. The air conditioning had already turned it into a refrigerator. Lionel ordered himself a power drink of some sort: any number of health-giving fruits and vegetables compounded into an unappealing green slime. I noticed that he had pulled on a knitted beanie as he sat down. He had luxurious hair but it was thinning on top and he was probably self-conscious. I was longing for scrambled eggs, but the nearest they had was poached eggs on smashed avocado with sourdough toast, none of which had the slightest appeal. I settled for a cappuccino.

We took a table by the window.

'I'm afraid I've only got half an hour,' Lionel said.

'It's very kind of you to see me.'

'Not at all, Sue. It's so awful about Cess.' He sounded almost too genuine to be genuine. 'Is there any news?'

'I'm afraid not.'

'That's terrible. And how are you involved in all this? Are you a friend of the family?'

'Not exactly. Lawrence Treherne asked me to help.' I didn't want to go into all that again and Lionel had already said we only had half an hour so I moved on swiftly, explaining how

Cecily's disappearance might be connected to Frank Parris's murder eight years before.

'Frank Parris!' He let out a low whistle. 'When I got your text, I wondered how I could help. I haven't been back to Branlow Hall since I left. I'll be straight up with you, Sue. I couldn't stand the place! I was glad to get out.'

'But you were there for quite a while, Lionel. Four years.'

He smiled at that. 'You've done your homework. Actually, it was three years and nine months. I took over the new spa once it was finished and that was cool. State-of-the-art equipment, everything brand new, great pool. I had some decent clients, too ... especially the ones from outside. But the pay was lousy and although I was doing personal training the Trehernes only paid me twenty-five per cent of the fee. They were shit employers. And let me tell you, sometimes the whole place was more like a madhouse than a smart hotel. Stefan was OK. And I got on with some of the kitchen staff. But I couldn't stand the rest of them.'

'I don't suppose you had a client called Melissa Conway?' I don't know why I asked about her. It had come as a surprise to me when James had mentioned she was living in Woodbridge and on the memory stick Cecily had said that she used the spa.

'Melissa? Yes, there was a lady called Melissa – she was in all the time. But her name was Melissa Johnson, I think. She rented a house on the estate.'

That was her, but she had gone back to her maiden name.

'Why do you want to know about her?' Lionel asked.

'She was married to Alan Conway,' I said.

'Oh! I get it. Well, since you mention it, she actually came in on the Wednesday or the Thursday evening before it happened. I remember because she was in a foul mood. No fun at all.'

'Do you know what had upset her?'

He shrugged. 'No idea.'

'So how did you end up at Branlow Hall?' I asked. 'How did you get the job?'

'Yeah, well, I didn't know what I was walking into. I came to London from Perth about eleven years ago. That's Perth, Australia, of course. My mother was English. I rented a room in Earls Court and got a job as a personal trainer. I was only twenty but I'd done a CEC course at a uni in Perth and I was lucky. I landed on my feet. I had a few private clients and they recommended me to others. Even so, London's an expensive place and I had a devil of a job keeping my head above water. You have no idea of the sort of stuff I got up to! Then I was training this guy and he mentioned he'd just got back from Branlow Hall and they were looking for someone to run their spa. It seemed a good way to earn some cash, so I went for an interview and I got it.'

'Who was the client who recommended you?' I asked.

'I don't remember.'

'Were all your clients men?'

'No. They split about fifty-fifty. Why do you ask?'

'No reason. Go on. Why were the Trehernes such bad employers – apart from the pay?'

'Well, the pay was the main thing, but they really made you put in the hours. Ten hours a day, six days a week. I'm not even sure that's legal, is it? And there were no perks.

Everything you ate in the hotel you had to pay for and although the food was cheap, they gave you zero discount in the bar. You weren't even allowed to go in if there were any guests there.

'And that thing they were doing with crims! The Youth Offender Programme, they called it, but that wasn't what it was about. It was the pits. They were paying Stefan way under the minimum wage and he was on call literally twenty-four hours a day. He was meant to be general maintenance but they had him doing all the shit jobs, including the toilets, the gutters on the roof, the trash … you name it. He got really sick once and they didn't even want to give him the day off. They had him over a barrel, you see. If he complained, they could throw him out. He was Romanian. He had a prison record. He wasn't going to get another job – and certainly not without a reference from them. They knew that. They were bastards.

'And then there was Lisa Treherne.' He shook his head in admiration. 'The older daughter. She was a real piece of work.'

'She accused him of stealing.'

'She knew he wasn't a thief. That was Natasha.'

'The maid?'

'Yes. Everyone knew that. She was shameless! Shake hands and check you're still wearing your watch. But Lisa was playing the same power game as her dad. She wanted Stefan.'

'Wanted him … how?'

'How do you think?' Lionel looked at me disdainfully. 'Lisa had the hots for him. A nice hunk of twenty-two-year-old Eastern European flesh. She couldn't keep her eyes off him.'

Could I trust what Lionel was telling me? According to him, Melissa was angry, Lawrence was crooked, Stefan was exploited and Lisa was rapacious. He didn't have a good word to say about anyone. And yet I thought back to the meeting I'd had with Lisa in the dining room at Branlow Hall. She'd been fairly vengeful herself. *'Hiring Stefan Codrescu was a mistake from the very start. I said so at the time, although nobody listened to me.'* And what was it her father had said? *'You liked him to start with. You spent lots of time with him.'* I'd made a note of the contradiction. Perhaps Lionel had just explained it.

'For what it's worth, Lisa tried it on with me as well,' he continued. 'She was always in and out of the spa, and I'm telling you, mate, the sort of workout she wanted didn't involve anything I'd been taught in Perth.'

'Did she have a relationship with Stefan?' Even as I asked the question, I thought it was unlikely. Surely, if they had been sleeping together, it would have come out at the trial.

Lionel shook his head. 'I wouldn't call it a relationship. Stefan didn't fancy her any more than I did.' He pointed at his mouth. 'You know, she had that scar, and even without it she wasn't exactly Miranda Kerr. But they were having sex, if that's what you mean. The poor bugger couldn't say no to her! After all, she was more or less running the hotel. She had complete power over him.'

'Did he talk to you about it?'

'No. He never talked about that sort of stuff. But he was always miserable when she was around and one time I actually saw them together.'

Another couple of people had come into the café. Lionel leaned forward conspiratorially.

'It happened about two or three weeks before the murder,' he said. 'I'd finished at the spa and I was doing a quick run around the grounds. It was a warm night. Beautiful. There was a full moon. So I ran and did some stretches and then I decided to do some chin-ups. There was a tree I liked to use. It had a branch at the perfect height. It was in this wood — near to Oaklands, the cottage where Melissa lived, as a matter of fact. So there I was, making my way along, when suddenly I heard noises and the next thing I knew, there they were the two of them, him on top of her, both of them stark naked in the grass.'

'Are you sure it was Lisa and Stefan?'

'That's a fair question, Sue. It was night and there was a distance between us, and at first I got the idea it was Aiden having it away with his future sister-in-law, which would have been quite a laugh. But I'd worked out with Aiden and he's got this big tattoo on his shoulder. He always called it his cosmic snake, but to me it just looked like a giant tadpole!' He laughed. 'Whoever the guy was out there, it wasn't Aiden. He had bare skin – I'd have easily seen a tattoo in the moonlight.

'Anyway, I didn't want to hang around like some kind of perv, whoever it was out there, so I started to move away. And of course you're going to guess what happened. I only stepped on a branch and the bloody thing went off like a gunshot. Well, that stopped them. The guy looked round and I saw his face as clearly as I'm seeing you now. It was definitely Stefan.'

'Did he see you?'

'I don't think so.'

'You never talked to him about it?'

'Are you kidding?'

I thought it through. 'But I don't understand,' I said. 'Lisa fired him a couple of weeks later. If they were having sex, why would she do that?'

'I wondered about that. But my guess is that he'd told her to get lost. What she was doing was exploitation, no more, no less. Maybe he threatened to put in a complaint.'

I still hadn't heard from Stefan Codrescu and I wondered how long it would take for my letter to reach him in jail. There was still the question of whether he would agree to see me, but it was critical that the two of us should meet. I needed to know everything that had happened between him and Lisa Treherne. She wasn't going to say anything. Only he could tell me the truth.

'You were with him on the Friday night,' I said. 'He got drunk at the party.'

'That's right.' Lionel glanced at the clock on the wall. We had been talking for twenty minutes of our allotted half-hour. He drained his protein shake, leaving a green half-moon on his upper lip. 'That wasn't like Stefan. He could usually hold his liquor. But of course he'd just been fired, so maybe he was drowning his sorrows.'

'You took him back to his room.'

'That would have been about ten o'clock. We walked over to the stable block, which is where they put us up. I had the room next to his. I said goodnight and we both went to bed. I was pretty knackered myself, actually.'

'What time did you get to sleep?'

'I guess about ten or fifteen minutes later – but before you ask, I didn't hear anything. I'm a heavy sleeper. If Stefan got up and went into the hotel, I'm afraid I can't help you. All I can tell you is that he was lying on his bed when I left.'

'Did you see him the next day?'

'No. I was in the spa. He was helping with the wedding.'

'Do you believe he killed Frank Parris?'

He had to think about that. Eventually, he nodded. 'Yeah. Probably. I mean, the police found plenty of evidence and I know he was broke. He did a lot of online gambling. All these Romanians do. He often asked me to bail him out before he got paid at the end of the month.'

He looked at the clock again and got to his feet. Our time was up.

'I hope you can help him, Sue,' he said. 'Because actually, I quite liked him and I think what happened to him was pretty crook. And I hope you find Cecily. Do they have any idea what happened to her?'

'Not yet.' There was one last thing I wanted to ask. 'You said that, at first, you thought it might be Aiden with Lisa in the wood. Was that because he was usually promiscuous?'

'Promiscuous! That's a funny word to use. You mean did he fool around?' Lionel gave me a crooked smile. 'I don't know anything about his marriage, and when I saw those two people out there I don't know why it popped into my head that it might be him. Maybe he and Cecily were happy together and maybe they weren't – but I'll tell you one thing. I don't think Aiden would've dared go behind her back. I mean, she was the one who'd found him and brought him up from London, and in her own way Cecily was as tough as her sister. If she'd found out he was cheating on her, she'd have had his balls for breakfast.'

We shook hands. Another trainer had come into the café, also in Lycra, and I watched the two of them give each other a man hug, bumping chests and rubbing each other's back.

I still wasn't sure that I liked Lionel Corby. Could I believe the version of events that he had presented to me? I wasn't sure about that either.

Michael Bealey (Lunch)

Michael J. Bealey was a busy man.

His PA had rung to say that drinks at Soho House would no longer work but could I meet him for lunch at twelve thirty? Lunch turned out to be a sandwich and a cup of coffee at a Prêt just around the corner from his flat on the King's Road, but that was fine by me. I wasn't sure if Michael would have had enough conversation for a two-course meal. He had always been a man of few words, despite having published millions of them. The "J." on his business card was important to him, by the way. It was said that he had known both Arthur C. Clarke and Philip K. Dick and had adapted his own name as a sort of tribute to them both. He was well known as an expert on their work and had written long articles that had been published in *Constellations* (which he had also edited at Gollancz) and *Strange Horizons*.

He was already there when I arrived, scrolling through a typescript on his iPad. There was something mole-like about the way he worked, hunched forward as if he was trying to burrow his way into the screen. I had to remind myself that he was about the same age as me. His grey hair, glasses and old-fashioned suit added an extra ten years, which he seemed to embrace. There are some men who are never really young, who don't even want to be.

'Oh, hello, Susan!' He didn't get up. He wasn't the kissing sort, not even a peck on the cheek. But he did at least fold the cover over his iPad and smile at me, blinking in the sun. He already had a coffee and a Bakewell tart, which was sitting on the paper bag it had come in. 'What can I get you?' he asked.

'Actually, I'm all right, thank you.' I had glanced at the rather depressing muffins and pastries on offer and hadn't been tempted. Anyway, I wanted to get this over with.

'Well, do help yourself to a piece of this.' He pushed the tart towards me. 'It's quite good.'

That clipped speech. I remembered it so well. He was like an actor in one of those plays from between the wars where everyone talks for a long time but very little happens.

'How are you?' he asked.

'I'm very well, thank you.'

'And in Greece, I understand!'

'Crete, actually.'

'I've never been to Crete.'

'You should. It's beautiful.'

Even on a Sunday, the traffic trundled past on the King's Road, and I could smell dust and petrol in the air.

'So how are things?' I asked, snatching at the question to fill the silence.

He sighed and blinked several times. 'Well, you know, it's been one of those years.' It always was, where Michael was concerned. He'd turned gloom into an art form.

'I was pleased to see you picked up the Atticus Pünd series.' I was determined to be positive. 'And you kept my old
covers. Somebody gave me a copy the other day. I thought it
looked great.'

'It seemed both pointless and uneconomical to rejack-
et them.'

'Are they selling well?'

'They were.'

I waited for him to explain what he meant but he just sat
there, sipping whatever was in his paper cup. 'So what happened?' I asked eventually.

'Well, it was that business with David Boyd.'

I vaguely knew the name but couldn't place it. 'Who is
David Boyd?'

'The writer.'

There was another silence. Then, hesitantly, Michael continued. 'I actually brought him into the company so in a way
I suppose it was my fault. I bought his first book at Frank-
furt. A three-way auction, but we were lucky. One publisher
dropped out and the second wasn't overenthusiastic, so we
got it at a good price. We published the first book eighteen
months ago and the second last January.'

'Science fiction?'

'Not exactly. Cybercrime. Very well researched. Quite
well written. It's actually quite terrifying stuff. Big business,
fraud, politics, the Chinese. Disappointing sales, though.
I don't know what went wrong, but the first book underper-
formed and the second book was actually much weaker. At
the same time, he had an aggressive agent – Ross Simmons
at Curtis Brown – trying to tie us down to a new deal, so we

took a decision and let him go. Sad, but there you are. These things happen.'

Was that the end of the story? 'What *did* happen?' I asked.

'Well, he took umbrage. Not the agent. The writer. He felt we'd let him down, gone back on our word. It was all very unpleasant, but the worst of it was that he – actually, you're not going to believe this – but it seems that he hacked into the Hely Hutchinson Centre to get his revenge.'

A whole series of terrifying possibilities opened up before my eyes. I had read about Hely Hutchinson in the *Bookseller*: a brand-new, state-of-the-art distribution centre near Didcot in Oxfordshire. Two hundred and fifty thousand square feet. Robot technology. Sixty million books shipped every year.

It had been a nightmare, Michael explained. 'It was absolute chaos. We had the wrong titles being sent to the wrong bookstores. Orders got ignored. We had one customer who received thirty copies of the same Harlan Coben . . . one a day for a whole month. Other books just disappeared. If you tried to find them it was as if they had never been written. That included the reissues of *Atticus Pünd*.' He realised that he had managed several sentences in one go and stopped himself. 'Very annoying.'

'How long did this go on for?' I asked.

'It's still going on. We've got people in there now, sorting it out. The last two months were the worst. God knows what it's going to do to our sales and operating profit for this quarter!'

'I'm very sorry,' I said. 'Have you gone to the police?'

'The police are involved, yes. I really can't say any more than that. We've managed to keep it out of the press. I shouldn't really even be talking to you about it.'

Why was he talking to me about it? I guessed. 'I suppose this isn't a very good time to be approaching you,' I said. 'I mean, for a job.'

'I'd love to help you, Susan. I think you did a very good job with the Pünd novels – and I understand Alan Conway wasn't an easy man to work with.'

'You don't know the half of it.'

'What actually happened? At Cloverleaf Books?'

'It wasn't my fault, Michael.'

'I'm sure it wasn't.' He broke off a piece of Bakewell tart. 'But, of course, there were rumours.'

'The rumours weren't true.'

'Rumours very rarely are.' He popped the fragment into his mouth and waited until it had melted. He didn't chew or swallow. 'Look, I'm firefighting at the moment and I really can't help you. But I can put the word out and see. What are you looking for? Publisher? Editorial director?'

'I'll take anything.'

'How about freelance? Project by project?'

'Yes. That might work.'

'There might be something.'

Or there might not. That was it.

'Are you sure you won't have a coffee?' he asked.

'No. Thank you, Michael.'

He didn't dismiss me quite yet. To have done so would have been a humiliation. We talked for another ten minutes about the business, about the collapse of Cloverleaf, about

Crete. He finished his coffee and his pastry and then we part-
ed company without shaking hands because he had icing
sugar on his fingers. So much for the Ralph Lauren jacket!
The meeting had been a complete waste of time.

Craig Andrews (Dinner)

It was my third meal of the day and I still hadn't eaten.

This time, however, I was going to make up for it. Craig had taken me to an old-fashioned trattoria in Notting Hill, one of those places where the waiters wear black and white and the pepper grinders are about six inches too long. The pasta was home-made, the wine rough and reasonably priced and the tables a little too close together. It was exactly the sort of restaurant I liked.

'So what do you think?' he asked as we tucked into very good bruschetta with ripe tomatoes and thick leaves of fresh basil.

'The food? The restaurant?'

'The crime! Do you think they'll find Cecily Treherne?'

I shook my head. 'If she was going to turn up, I think she'd have done so by now.'

'So she's dead.'

'Yes.' I thought for a moment. I hated writing her off like that. 'Probably.'

'Do you have any idea who killed her?'

'It's complicated, Craig.' I tried to collect my thoughts. 'Let's start with the call that Cecily made to her parents. And let's assume that someone overheard her talking. I thought at first that she had telephoned from Branlow Cottage, in which case it could only have been Aiden or Eloise, the nanny. But actually she made the call from her office in the hotel and that widens the field.'

'How do you know?'

'Because Derek, the night manager, was there and he told me. "*I knew something was wrong when she made that phone call. She was so upset.*" That was what he said.'

'So he overheard her.'

'Yes. But Lisa Treherne had the office next door and she might have too. It could have been one of the guests. It could have been someone walking past the window outside.' I sighed. 'Here's the problem. If you accept that Cecily had to be silenced because she knew something about the death of Frank Parris, then it follows that whoever killed her killed him. But as far as I can tell, none of the people I've mentioned had ever met Frank before. Not Derek, not Aiden, not Lisa. None of them had any motive.'

'Could they have killed Cecily to protect someone else?'

'I suppose so. But who? Frank Parris had been in Australia. He turned up by chance on the weekend of the wedding and he had no connection whatsoever with Branlow Hall except that he had booked himself in for three days.' I drank some of the wine, which had rather pleasingly arrived at the table tucked into a straw basket. 'Funnily enough, I have found two people who had a proper motive for killing him. And they've lied to me! But the trouble is, they live outside the hotel and I can't see any way that they could have overheard Cecily making her telephone call.' I thought about it. 'Unless they happened to be there for a drink ... '

'Who are they?'

'Joanne and Martin Williams. Sister and brother-in-law of the deceased. They live in Westleton and Frank had a half-share in their house. That was the reason he was in Suffolk. He was going to force them to sell it.'

'How do you know they lied?'

'It was a small thing, really.'

It was Aiden who had first mentioned it. The marquee for the wedding had arrived late. It hadn't come to the hotel until Friday lunchtime. When Martin Williams was talking about his brother-in-law, he had said that Frank had complained about the wedding and in particular about the marquee, which spoiled the view of the garden. But he had also told me that Frank had come to the house early, after breakfast. So, putting two and two together, Frank couldn't possibly have seen the marquee.

On the other hand, Martin most certainly had. He must have gone to Branlow House sometime after Friday afternoon. Why? It was just possible that he wanted to find out which room Frank was in because he'd decided to kill him. Which would also explain Joanne's last words to me: *'Piss off and leave us alone.'* She knew what had happened and she was scared.

I told Craig all this and he smiled. 'That's very clever, Susan. Do you think this guy, Martin Williams, had it in him to kill his brother-in-law?'

'Well, as I say, he was the only one with any motive. Unless ... ' I hadn't meant to put my thoughts into words, but Craig was fascinated by the whole story and I knew I had to go on. 'Well, it's a crazy idea, but it has occurred to me that Frank might not have been the target.'

'Meaning?'

'First of all, he changed rooms. He was originally in room sixteen but apparently it was too modern for him. So they put him in room twelve.'

'Who went into room sixteen?'

'A retired headmaster called George Saunders. He taught at a local school. Bromeswell Grove. But suppose someone didn't know that. They knock on the door of room twelve in the middle of the night and he opens it and in the half-light they whack him on the head with a hammer and kill him before they know what they've done.'

'Would he have opened the door in the middle of the night?'

'That's a good point. But I've had another thought. Suppose this wasn't about Frank Parris or George Saunders or any of the guests. It could have been all about Stefan Codrescu. It seems that he was having an affair with Lisa Treherne and there was all sorts of sexual jealousy and anger bubbling away at Branlow Hall. Suppose someone wanted to frame him?'

'For murder?'

'Why not?'

'And just killed a guest at random?' He didn't need to inject so much scepticism into his voice. I wasn't sure I believed it myself. 'I can see why you need to talk to Stefan,' he said.

220

'If he ever gets back to me.'

'It may take a while. The prison system makes things as difficult as possible for everyone involved – inside and out. That's what it looks like, anyway.'

The main course came. We talked for a while about prisons.

When I'd first met Craig, four years earlier, he'd had the nervousness of all new writers; the sense that he needed to apologise for what he was doing. He had just turned forty, quite old to be starting out as a writer, although quite a bit younger than Alexander McCall Smith had been when he published his first major hit, *The No. 1 Ladies' Detective Agency*, and maybe that was partly in my mind when I took him on. He was also wealthy. He didn't show off, but his clothes, his car, the house in Ladbroke Grove, all told their own story. He had just left Goldman Sachs, where he'd headed up their UK Shares division. This information never appeared in his blurb.

I had assured him that *Jail Time* (as it eventually became) didn't need any apology and I had enjoyed working with him. His main character, Christopher Shaw, was a plain-clothes policeman, sent into maximum-security jails to get information from high-profile inmates, and this was a formula that had worked well for the first three books in the series.

'What got you interested in prisons?' I asked him now. We were getting to the end of the main course. We'd worked our way through the bottle of wine.

'Didn't I ever tell you?' I saw him hesitate. The lights from the candles were reflecting in his eyes. 'My brother was in prison.'

'I'm sorry ... ' I was surprised he had never told me before. The more cynical part of me could have used it as publicity.

'John was the chief executive of one of the high-street banks. He was trying to raise investment from Qatar – this was in 2008, just after the financial crisis. He was paying them sweeteners, which of course he didn't declare. The Serious Fraud Office went after him. And ... ' he waved a hand ' ... he got three years.'

'I shouldn't have asked.'

'No. It's OK. John was scared and stupid rather than greedy, and what happened to him made me rethink my whole career. It could just as easily have been me. And prison! I'm not saying he shouldn't have been punished, but prison is such a bloody waste of time. I'm convinced that one day people will look back on the twenty-first century and wonder how we could perpetuate such an absurd, Victorian idea. Do you want a dessert?'

'No.'

'Then let's have coffee at home.'

It was another warm night and we decided to walk back. I wondered if I had spoiled the evening by asking about his personal life, but it had actually brought us closer.

'Were you ever married?' he asked.

'No.' The question took me by surprise.

'Me neither. I came close a couple of times but it didn't work out, and now I suppose it's too late.'

'What are you talking about?' I said. 'You're not even fifty.'

'That's not what I mean. Who in their right mind would want to marry a writer?'

'I know lots of writers who are very happily married.'

'I was seeing someone last year. She was divorced, about my age. We shared a lot of interests. I really liked her. But I never allowed her anywhere near me ... not when I was working. And the trouble was, I was working all the time. In the end she got fed up with it and I can't blame her. When you're writing a book, the book is all that matters and some people can't accept that.'

We had reached his front door. He opened it and we went inside.

'Are you with anyone, Susan?' he asked.

That was the moment when everything changed. God knows, I've read enough romantic novels to recognise when subtext comes galloping over the horizon and I knew exactly what Craig was asking – or rather, I saw the invitation behind the question he had just put to me. It should have been obvious the moment I'd entered his swish bachelor's home or accepted dinner at that quaint local restaurant with its candles and its wine bottles in straw baskets.

The worst of it was that I didn't know how to answer.

I wasn't in Crete. I wasn't with Andreas. I was tempted. Why not? Craig represented a metropolitan lifestyle, parties, bestselling books ... everything, in fact, that I had left behind. He was also handsome, good company, civilised and rich. And if one little voice whispered in my ear that this was what I had been afraid of from the moment I had invited myself into his home, another reminded me that it was what I'd actually wanted and advised me to grab it with both hands.

'No. I was with someone but we broke up.'

That was what I wanted to say. That was what I could have said. It would have been so easy. But right then it wasn't true. Not yet. And maybe I didn't want it to be.

'Are you with anyone, Susan?' he asked

'Yes. Didn't I tell you? I'm engaged.'

I watched as he took that in. 'Congratulations,' he said. 'Who's the lucky man?'

'His name is Andreas. He's the co-owner of the hotel in Crete.'

'I have to say, it's the last thing I'd have expected you to get up to but that's wonderful. So – shall we have a coffee?'

'No, thanks. It's been a lovely evening, but I've got an early start if I'm going to get back to Suffolk.'

'Of course.'

'Thanks for dinner, Craig.'

'My pleasure.'

We were like two actors in a play, reciting lines that had been written by someone else. He gave me a peck on the cheek and then – *exit stage right* – I went upstairs on my own.

Page One

A large gin and tonic. A club sandwich held together by a cocktail stick flying a miniature Stars and Stripes. A packet of cigarettes. And the book.

I was ready.

I had driven back to Suffolk in time for lunch and after unpacking and taking a quick shower in my room, I had deposited myself at one of the wooden tables in the area outside the bar. I was right next to the stretch of grass – the east lawn – where Aiden and Cecily's wedding marquee had been pitched. The main entrance to the hotel was round the corner and I thought of Helen, the house manager (I imagined her as elderly and serious in a well-cut uniform), running breathlessly across the gravel to find Lawrence and tell him what Natasha had just found in room 12. How horrible it must have been for all of them that day! All the guests in their smart clothes, Aiden and Cecily married barely an hour, and then suddenly police cars and photographers and questions from the unlovely Detective

Superintendent Locke and finally the body brought out on a stretcher ...

The sun was shining but I shuddered. I'd have been more comfortable indoors, but I'm afraid reading and smoking have always gone together for me and even though it was a disgusting habit (the smoking, obviously) I needed to concentrate. The book was *Atticus Pünd Takes the Case*. It was the copy that Craig had given me in London. The time had finally come to confront not just the text but my memories of its creation. It felt strange. I was about to read one murder mystery while sitting inside another.

I had put off reading it for reasons that I have already explained. I was perfectly well aware of the identity of the killer in the novel and I remembered all the clues. I think it would be fair to say that a whodunnit is one of the very few forms of literature that rarely merit a second read.

But by now I had a good idea of what had happened at Branlow Hall on the 14th and 15th of June. I had met most of the characters involved. Alan Conway had come to the hotel. Perhaps he had even sat where I was sitting now. And he had seen something. *'They've got the wrong man.'* That was what he had said to James Taylor. He had come here in search of inspiration but he had left with much more. And yet he hadn't gone to the police. He had hidden the answer in his book. It was the only way to make sense of Cecily's disappearance and I was going to find it.

The paperback was in front of me. I ran my finger across the raised letters of the title, feeling them as if they were in Braille. It was extraordinary how much damage Alan Conway had managed to do in his career. *Magpie Murders* had almost killed me. Had this prequel killed Cecily Treherne?

I lit a cigarette. I turned to the first page.

I began to read.